THE DEVIL'S TREE

SUSAN MCCAULEY

Sophia,
Don't forget to turn
out the lights!
Susan McCauley

CELTIC SEA PUBLISHING

The Library of Congress has cataloged this work as follows:

McCauley, Susan

The Devil's Tree/ Susan McCauley

ISBN: 978-1-951069-00-1 (trade)

ISBN: 978-1-951069-01-8 (ebook)

For Alex who loves adventures and has grown to love fiction;
for Rick who supports me no matter what;
for Mom who has always believed in me;
for Dad who wasn't able to be here to see my debut novel in print;
I love you all.

CONTENTS

CHAPTER 1

I strapped on my seat belt and got ready for a wild ride. That's what Hunter gave me most weekends. Except tonight. Tonight he'd gone and ticked me off. I only got one Saturday night off a month, and instead of going out on a date, he was dragging me and our two best friends to the outskirts of town to snap photos of a haunted tree.

Yeah, a freakin' tree.

Hunter jammed his boot into the gas pedal and the engine of his F-150 roared to life. Thankfully, the truck was in park or we'd have shot straight through his daddy's newly painted white-picket fence. That would be bad. Real bad. His daddy would've come out screaming and waving his shotgun. The man was already three sheets gone. Whiskey. Wild Turkey, I think. At least that's what Hunter's mama always bought when I worked the night shift at the Food Mart. Same as what my mama drank.

Hunter clapped his calloused hand on my knee, high enough that his fingers could tickle my thigh beneath my denim skirt. Man, he really knew how to get me going. I tried not to smile. Naughty boy.

"Why can't we just go to Mojo's and grab a burger

instead of going to some haunted tree?" I whined, pretending I didn't care about how hot and tingly his hand felt on my thigh. I pulled my leg away and shoved a few stray hairs back into my ponytail instead of giving in to his efforts to ruin my sour mood. I deserved a little sour, didn't I? He was dragging me on a freakin' ghost hunt. But Hunter just grinned. He knew me too well. I'd do just about anything for that boy.

"I promised Dylan I'd take him, that's why." Hunter gave me a melt-my-heart smile that promised he'd make it up to me later.

I rolled my eyes. What on God's good earth did Hunter even have in common with Dylan? Hunter was tall, buff, good-looking, liked sports. Dylan? Skinny, pale, glasses, computer nerd all the way. Total geek. Even if he was kind of nice.

The boys had been in diapers together. Yeah, that long. Still, I understood their friendship just about as much as I understood why Keisha and Dylan were together. And Lord only knew what Dylan's daddy thought of his son dating a black girl. It was kinda like what Hunter's mama thought when she first found out he was dating me. "White trash," she'd called me. Yeah, Keisha had to deal with racist crap and that sucked, but she acted like my life with a drunk mama in a trailer park on welfare was some kind of cakewalk by comparison. Like she would know. At least she had two parents with steady paychecks. Two parents who loved her.

Keisha and I had been best friends until Dylan came along. I swear that girl's as jealous as a tamale without hot sauce. I couldn't understand it. I wasn't the sort of girl to steal my friend's boyfriend—even if I was interested in him, which I wasn't. She *knew* that. Besides, I was with Hunter. Always would be. Next summer we'd leave this town together and never look back. We'd get scholarships for college, or we'd save up enough to get out. Either way, we were going to leave this dead-end town and my dead-end life. No more white trash comments from his mama or anyone else. I snorted, flipped open the sun visor mirror, grabbed lipstick out of my purse, and precisely applied.

Ck-ck-ck-ck-ck! Five loud taps made me drop my lipstick and about made me crap my pants.

Hunter laughed and hit the button to roll down my window.

"Dammit, Keisha. Why'd you do that?" I scraped a waxy red lump off my skirt. "That was my Siren in Scarlet. You owe me a tube."

Keisha batted her totally fake lashes at me. "Next time I'm at Walmart."

"Whatever." Still, that lipstick cost me an hour's pay. She'd better get me a new one. Or get her rich boyfriend to. Dylan's daddy was the richest man in town, even if he was a racist bastard. I still couldn't believe Keisha was willing to put up with that to date Dylan.

Keisha opened my door, shoved my seat forward with me in it, and climbed in back. *I swear. . . .*

"Sorry, Kaitlyn," Dylan mumbled, eyes darting to my boobs that were crunched to my knees.

"Don't be so damned polite." I shoved my seat back with a snap, making Dylan fall into his seat. "If I hadn't been dating this jerk for the last two years," I said and hooked a thumb toward Hunter, "I'd never have agreed to go on this stupid ghost hunt."

Hunter snorted. "Kaitlyn's in a bit of a *mood*." I shot him a glare. "You're beautiful even when you're pissed at me." He chuckled and put the truck in reverse, then tore out of his daddy's gravel drive.

"It's not a ghost hunt," Dylan called out from the backseat, then flipped open a page in his notebook and scribbled something I couldn't see. "It's the Devil's Tree."

"Ghost hunt. Devil's Tree. Whatever." I dropped the damaged lipstick tube into my bag and snapped it closed. Dylan always sounded way smarter than everyone else. Being in Mensa, that smart person club, he probably was way smarter, but still.

"It's no joke, Kaitlyn." Keisha leaned over Dylan to look at me in the visor mirror, her doe-like eyes serious. "We've all heard stories. People've been run off the road near that tree. Some of the old folks in town say if you stand out there long enough, you'll hear moaning at night. They think it's the spirits of all those black folks the whites in town lynched way back when. Some say it wasn't an accident Old Joe died on that road right after trying to cut down the tree."

"It won't work trying to scare me." I had no room in my life for superstition or ghost stories. My daddy'd always told me that stories like that were nonsense. Silly tales made up to scare kids away from other people's property. I shrugged. "I'm only going 'cause I've got nothing better to do on a Saturday night." *Liar.* I'd much rather be having a burger and flirting a drink out of the bartender at Mojo's. Even though Keisha and I were seventeen, the bartenders at Mojo's tended to ignore that little detail for pretty faces. Not that I'd drink it, mind you. With Mama like she was, drinking wasn't high on my to-do list. The point was getting it.

Hunter turned out of his neighborhood and headed toward the old farm road that would take us to the Devil's Tree.

Rocks crunched and churned under our tires, and I turned around to get a better look at Dylan's fancy camera. "So, if it's not haunted, then why the camera?"

"I didn't say it wasn't haunted," Dylan said. Something in his serious eyes made me shudder.

I turned back around in my seat and gazed out my window at the darkening sky. At the bright greens of summer fading in the twilight. The hum of cicadas buzzed and shivered through the glass. A perfect summer sound. The sound of a warm, humid, sleepy summer night.

"I think it is haunted," Dylan said, his voice quiet but certain. "But I'm not after ghosts. I want to learn more about the tree. I'm hoping that the pictures we get and whatever we experience will give us a better idea of what happened there. The town newspaper has already agreed to publish an article if we find anything new. Except for Old Joe's accident, they've got nothing but rumors and vague reports. And most are decades old."

"Yeah," Keisha said. "We have important questions to answer. Like why do leaves never grow on it? And why does snow never fall there?" Well look at her, getting all in on her boyfriend's obsession.

"Of course snow doesn't fall on it, Keisha. We live in southeast Texas. Snow barely falls anywhere down here." She scowled and I looked out my window, not so thrilled about being bitchy with her—but seriously? Suddenly the world revolves around what your boyfriend's interested in? Besides, the good folks of Harland had been asking those questions for years. "I don't see how you're gonna figure it all out, when Old Joe and every other geezer who's ever gone to that tree has come up empty-handed."

"Or dead." Hunter smiled, gunned the accelerator, and hit a pothole.

Keisha squealed and we all popped half out of our seats. Why did I put up with him? Maybe because he was a good kisser. Maybe because of his hot muscles. Maybe because he was the only person in my life who thought I was more than just a cute body with a drunk mother. I don't know. I huffed and let my arms fall crisscross over my chest, still pissed that we weren't going to hang out at Mojo's.

I peeked at Dylan and Keisha in the rearview mirror. "None of those people were Dylan," Keisha said and draped an arm around Dylan's shoulder. "He has the equipment. We're bound to find something new, right, baby?" she cooed, which made Dylan blush and me want to vomit.

I shrugged and glared at Hunter, who only laughed. "Lighten up, babe." His hand found its way back to my knee. "It'll be fun." His finger danced in a little circle on my thigh. "Maybe when we're done we'll still have time to grab a burger, or something else." His voice dipped in that low, sexy way it does when he wants more than a burger.

I shoved his hand away, trying to keep a smile from busting out on my lips. "Keep your hands on the wheel."

The Devil's Tree wasn't too far from town. Just a few miles down the old dirt road, then about fifty feet off the shoulder in an area that was called a state park, but looked like nothing more than an abandoned field with scattered oaks.

Then I saw it. Coming closer through the dark. The beams of our headlights illuminated its skeletal limbs that stuck out at odd angles, a length of chain-link fence wrapped around its trunk maybe in an attempt to stop crazy folks from coming out here to try and hack it down.

Hunter pulled to a stop and let the engine idle. We stared. There were a couple other oak trees nearby, but they had leaves. Not the Devil's Tree. Nope. Just dead limbs and gnarly roots. It looked like something straight out of one of the scary movies we watched at Hunter's house some weekends.

"Well, we're here." Hunter turned the key and the engine died. He opened his door. I heard Hunter's breathing and the squeak of Keisha squirming on the vinyl backseat, but the hum of cicadas was suspiciously missing.

I closed my eyes and listened. There were no sounds nearby. No people. No cars. If I listened closely, I could hear a few birds in the distance. The bellow of a frog.

My eyes snapped open and I looked at the deeply shadowed oak. A chain dangled from one of its middle branches. Red spray-painted graffiti decorated its trunk with the words *Stay Back!* I could even see a few hack marks toward the base, barely showing from beneath the chain link. Those must've been the marks Old Joe had carved into the trunk when he'd tried to rid us all of the fiendish tree. The thought of Old Joe's broken body made me shiver.

The day after he tried to hack down the Devil's Tree, they'd found his car crashed in the ravine, his body bloated from a night in the river. But they never found out what caused the crash.

"Come on then." Dylan pushed my seat, nudging me to let him out. "Let's go have a look." He stuffed the notebook in his backpack and grabbed the camera.

I swung my feet out of the cab and felt my three-inch heels sink into the muck. This was so not my thing. I might work at the Food Mart, but I liked going out to restaurants and the mall and having fun. Not going camping or walking through muddy fields in the summer heat. Hunter owed me. Big time. So did Dylan. "Right," I said, and took a step forward, trying to balance on the balls of my feet so my heels wouldn't squish into the mud.

Dylan climbed out behind me, then Keisha. "Here." Dylan handed Keisha a thermometer. "You can monitor the area for temperature fluctuations."

"Ooo, sounds important." Keisha smiled and took the gauge like she'd just been handed a diamond ring.

Oh, please. I rolled my eyes and shivered despite the muggy summer breeze.

Hunter slammed his door, walked around the front of the truck, and slung an arm around my waist. He pulled me toward him, his warm, musky scent drawing me closer.

I couldn't help but smile. He was hotter than a goat's butt in a pepper patch.

Dylan turned on his fancy digital camera and began snapping shots, the flash popping like blinding bursts of lightning.

Hunter shielded his face with his free arm. "Aw, man . . . do you really need the flash? We can't see anything."

Dylan lowered his camera. "It's dark out, Hunt." To him, Hunter was Hunt. Always. I hated it. "I won't get much without a flash. But I may try the infrared setting once we get closer to the tree. Come on."

Despite my flash-assaulted eyes, I could see Dylan's perfect white teeth grinning like a demented jack-o'-lantern in the moonlight. Boy, he really did get off on this stuff.

Hunter tugged me forward, his warm body shielding me from the strange, cool breeze that had kicked up.

I stumbled in a hole, but Hunter caught me.

"Damn. I broke a heel." I bent down and felt the heel of my right shoe dangling. These things cost me nearly an entire shift's pay and we had too many bills for me to go and buy new ones.

"Whoever heard of wearing high heels on an expedition?" Keisha said.

"People who didn't know they were going on an expedition when they were asked out on their only free

Saturday night this month," I snapped. Ugh, sometimes she made my skin crawl. She'd say anything to please Dylan. Fact is, before they got together this past fall, Keisha never wore anything but heels. I hate it when girls change who they are just for a boy. At least Hunter knew who I was and where I came from. And he loved me despite it.

Screw it. I ripped the heel off my damaged shoe and handed Hunter my other one. "Would ya mind?"

He looked at me, his hazel eyes gray in the moonlight. "Seriously?"

I shrugged. "It's not like I can wear one without the other. Go ahead. Break it."

"Alright, but I'll buy you a new pair." And with one hefty snap, that's just what he did, then tossed the broken wedge off into the dark field. I slipped my second heel-less shoe onto my foot and started walking. Huh, they were actually more comfortable this way, but I'd never admit it.

"Slow down, babe." Hunter caught up with me, draping his denim jacket over my shoulders. Dylan and Keisha trailed behind.

"How long is this gonna take?" I was about ten feet from the tree when something stopped me. I'm not sure what, but this feeling came over me. A sort of uneasy feeling like dread leaking into my gut. "I—I don't want to go any closer." My words came out in a whisper soft as the breeze.

"I thought you didn't believe in ghosts?" Dylan asked and pushed a button on his camera. I scowled, but he didn't seem to notice. "I'm switching over to infrared so I don't blind you guys."

Hunter took off around the backside of the tree.

"Where you going?" I asked, not wanting him to leave me, but sure as hell not willing to follow.

"Gotta take a piss."

I took a step forward. Stopped. There was that feeling again. Like something died inside me. "Don't you dare do it near the tree," I screeched, surprised at the fear in my voice.

Hunter laughed. "I'll piss right on the damn thing. See if it stirs up any spirits for Dylan."

Keisha scowled, and Dylan just kept shooting pictures.

If ghosts did exist, Hunter would likely piss them off enough that they'd come scare the living hell out of us. *I don't believe in ghosts. I don't believe in ghosts.* That's what I kept telling myself.

Click. Click. Click.

Dylan kept shooting photos.

Everything went silent, except for the pitter-pat of Hunter's pee splattering against tree bark and the click, click, clicking of Dylan's camera.

A gust kicked up and the dead branches rustled overhead. Keisha scooted closer to me and shivered. She kept her eyes locked on the temperature gauge. White puffs billowed out of her mouth with each breath. It reminded me of when we were seven years old in the neighbor's haunted house. We'd screamed and cried and held on to each other for dear life. I loved Keisha, even if she was a pain in my backside sometimes.

That's when I noticed I was shaking. Not shaking scared. Shaking cold. The temperature had dropped by at least twenty degrees.

"Hunter?"

No answer.

"Kaitlyn, do you see this?" Keisha's voice was stretched thin, like a balloon overfilled with water, and she showed me the digital thermometer. "The temperature just dropped from eighty-five to sixty."

Dylan kept snapping photos. "Just keep watching the gauge." He walked around the tree, near where Hunter had been peeing.

Keisha gave me a quick I'm-scared-as-hell glance and followed Dylan.

Click. Click. Click.

"It's even colder over here. It's dropped into the fifties." Keisha's voice broke the dark silence, and I wished she hadn't left my side.

A deep moan like a tree branch breaking or a man dying filled the air and a scream escaped my throat.

"Let's go." I stumbled forward and grabbed Hunter's arm. Hunter stood there, transfixed, a strange glaze over his eyes. Keisha's mouth was agape. Dylan kept snapping pictures.

"Let's go," I screamed, but no one moved. "What's wrong with you people?"

I pulled Hunter away from the tree. Away from the deep moan that echoed in the marrow of my bones. I ran to the truck, threw open the door, and leapt in.

They were all moving now. Fear lit Keisha's face as she jumped in the backseat. Hunter, breathing heavy, slid into the driver's seat, put the key into the ignition, and revved the engine.

The moan grew louder and my body trembled, adrenaline shooting through my veins.

"Where's Dylan?" Keisha sounded on the brink of hysteria.

Dylan's back was to us, camera raised, but useless. He gaped at the tree.

"Dammit, Dylan. Get your ass in the car. Now!" Hunter roared.

Dylan snapped out of his trance, took one more shot, then lumbered toward us. Face white, sheened in sweat, he climbed in just as a frigid, not so Texas wind ripped through the car.

I slammed the door shut and hit the lock button. "Go," I yelled. "Go now!"

The wheels of Hunter's truck spun on the gravel shoulder before gaining traction and we shot back onto the road, headed toward town.

I sagged against the truck window and closed my eyes, the cool glass soothing me. I swallowed. I didn't believe in ghosts. But something was there. Something real. Something evil.

Hunter's ragged breath beat against the stale air in the cab. Keisha sobbed. Dylan was silent. I opened my eyes.

Hunter's gaze was transfixed on the rearview mirror.

Lights were reflected there. Headlights.

"Where'd that car come from?" My voice sounded like a stranger's, deep and totally freaked out.

"I don't know . . ." Hunter's voice was frantic, afraid. "It just—just appeared. Out of nowhere."

"Oh, God . . . Oh, God . . . Oh, God." Keisha's voice rose with each syllable. "It's just like what happened to the boys who came to visit from up north . . . Just before they were run off the road and died!"

"Shut up, Keisha," Hunter growled, and gunned the accelerator.

"Just get us back to town," Dylan said, forcing calm into his voice.

The rattling thrum of an engine revved behind us. I looked in my side-view mirror. A black truck had pulled up right on our tail.

"Go faster," I whispered. "Can't you go any faster?"

"I'm trying."

The speedometer reached sixty-five, but the road

ahead curved. The posted speed was thirty-five. Hunter'd have to hit the brakes or we'd crash.

"Slow down," I screamed.

"I can't." Hunter's white-knuckled hands gripped the steering wheel. "My foot—it's—it's stuck on the accelerator."

"Oh, God," Keisha cried.

Tears streamed down my face. My hand slid over the door lock. Maybe I should jump?

The trees whipped by. No way. I couldn't jump. I'd never survive. Hands shaking, I tugged on my seat belt. Buckled it. Crap—Hunter didn't have his seat belt on. Did anybody else?

The speedometer read seventy. Hunter took the curve.

A big tree. Coming fast.

Time slowed.

Our tires squealed and my world turned upside down. Glass. Metal. Wood. Splintered. Screaming. Broken.

Silence.

CHAPTER 2

MY PULSE POUNDED IN MY EARS.

Drip. Drip. Drip.

Slowly my vision cleared. I hung upside down from my seat, wet hair dangling in front of my eyes. I turned my neck and pain shot down my shoulder. My face burned and I tasted the bitter salt of blood on my lips.

I smelled gasoline and pushed back the puke that threatened to spew out.

"Hunter?"

No answer.

What if the thing that chased us was still out there? Waiting?

"Hunter?" I focused on him and my voice cracked with panic.

Hunter was crumpled against the broken windshield. I reached forward and tried to touch him. Something dark and wet and sticky covered his skin. Blood. I started crying again. I scrabbled for my seat-belt buckle, but couldn't find it. My hands kept groping.

"Dylan? Keisha?"

Dylan moaned, but didn't answer.

"We gotta get out of the car." Away from the fumes. Away from whatever was chasing us.

There. My shaky fingers brushed the buckle and I pushed. The seat belt released me and I fell onto the smashed windshield next to Hunter. I let my hand graze his cheek. Still warm. Ragged breathing. Thank God.

I reached for my door. Pushed. Being upside down, it was jammed shut. I aimed my heel-less shoed feet toward the passenger-side window and kicked. The glass cracked, but stayed intact. I kicked again and cleared a space, then I twisted around to face the busted-out window and looked into the backseat. "We've gotta get out of here."

"Keisha." Dylan shook her bloody shoulder. "Keisha!" He shook her harder. "She's not breathing. Kaitlyn, help me!" Panic laced his voice. The smell of gas grew stronger, mingled with the metallic scent of blood.

"We'll go around to the other side of the truck to get them out." I slithered over broken glass, sharp against my skin.

Dylan stopped, eyes wide. Wild. "What—what if it's out there?"

Fear congealed in my veins, and I tried to clear my head. "We don't have a choice," I said, sounding way braver than I felt. "We have to get out. Now." I pulled myself forward, a few shards of metal slicing my palms and shredding my knees.

Dylan climbed out after me. Blood smeared his pale face; his normally pristine shirt was torn and dirty.

I crawled around the mangled wreck to Hunter's door, but Dylan pushed past me and grabbed Keisha.

Whoosh. A strange sucking wind whipped my hair into my mouth. Salt and blood and smoke.

I grabbed Dylan under his arms and yanked him backwards. Hard. We both fell, the pain of the concrete exploding up my tailbone and into my spine.

Boom!

"Hunter!" I screamed and lurched forward, the heat searing my face. My gut twisting in agony. I crawled toward the twisted, burning heap that had been Hunter's pride and joy. Tears burned a cut on my face. My legs ached as I dragged them across the ground.

Then Dylan's arms were around me. Solid. Real. Alive.

Sirens blared in the distance. Someone must've seen. Must've called. They were coming. But they were too late. We were all too late.

His wet cheek pressed against mine. "We can't help them. We can't . . ."

I pulled against his too strong grip and screamed and screamed and screamed. But he didn't let me go. I collapsed into him, sobbing into his skinny chest. Hating him for being alive. Wishing he was dead instead of Hunter.

———

THREE RAPS on my door drew my attention from the reflection in the mirror. My reflection. My face was thinner than normal, a still-healing cut along my lip and chin, a purple-blue bruise on my cheek, my blond hair pulled back in a ponytail. I used to hate ponytails. Now I didn't seem to care about doing my hair. Or makeup. Or much of anything else.

I'd wanted to get gussied up for Keisha and Hunter's funerals. So I'd managed to put on a dab of what remained of my Siren in Scarlet lipstick before tossing the tube in the trash. The lipstick was for Keisha. And for Hunter, I slipped on a little black dress he'd liked. Maybe he could see it now. That made me smile. Maybe Hunter was still alive somewhere—even if he wasn't with me. The clothes clung to me like the cobwebs in my brain. But staring at myself, I only saw a ghost. A ghost of the girl I'd been just days ago. They were gone. Dead. And somehow a piece of me had gone and died right along with them. All those dreams about Hunter and me leaving this loser town next summer, leaving behind my trailer park life, gone. Now there was nothing. Nothing but work and my drunk mama. Nothing but broken dreams.

Bang. Bang. Bang.

Mama usually wasn't so persistent unless she was out of whiskey. She knew I didn't want to talk. "What is it?" My voice was gravelly. I'd hardly spoken since the accident. "I already put out your breakfast, Mama."

"It's me."

That voice made me cringe. Dylan.

"What are you doing here?" I kept my back to my bedroom door, just staring at the stranger looking back at me in the mirror.

The door creaked open and Dylan walked in. In his funeral suit, he looked too dapper to be Dylan. I hated that he was here. He'd never been to our trailer before. At least not inside. But I was too exhausted to put up a fight or to give a crap. My life was ruined, so he might as well see me. The real me. Trashy home. Drunk Mama. Barely two cents to call my own. The me that Hunter knew and loved anyway. I was sort of surprised Dylan had even come inside. And yet, here he was.

Right arm in a sling, he held the camera in his left hand. "I thought you might want to look at these with me."

I stiffened. I never wanted to see Dylan or his pictures. Not at the hospital. Not at the funeral. Not here. Not ever.

But I was curious. Who or what had chased us? Would the pictures tell us anything? "I'm surprised the camera survived . . ." My voice trailed off, my choice of words not so good.

Dylan stiffened, shrugged. "It did."

"And you haven't looked at them yet? The pictures?"

He shook his head, his lips trembling. "Maybe it'll help give us some closure before we go."

I sighed and turned to face him. "Give me the camera, then." I held out my hands, took it, and sat weakly on the bed, my cut and bruised knees and tailbone still aching.

Dylan just stood there, gaze stuck to the floor like a fly in honey.

I patted the bed beside me, glad he was here, but not glad at the same time. "Have a seat."

"They shouldn't have died." His voice quivered. "If—if I hadn't—if I hadn't had to go to that—stupid tree."

"Stop." Camera in my lap, I held up my hand. I didn't have to like Dylan being alive and Hunter being dead. But I wasn't one to let people wallow in guilt. "Stop it right now. It's not your fault they're . . ." *Dead.* I couldn't say the word. I could barely even think it. Like if I didn't think it then maybe it wouldn't be true. "It's not your fault they're gone. Hunter had a choice. So did Keisha. So did I. We chose to go with you. We chose to go to that stupid tree." The same guilt that was eating at Dylan was eating at me, but I forged on. "And if we'd stayed to pull them out of the truck, we'd all be having funerals today."

Dylan looked up, and I was surprised to see how pretty his eyes were. Crystal blue. Like the aquamarine ring Mama'd sold when we couldn't pay rent right after Daddy left. Huh. I'd never noticed his were so nice before.

He slowly walked over and sat beside me on the edge of my tiny, unmade bed. I held the camera to him.

"You do it." He nodded toward the power button. "It should go back to the beginning of that day."

I swallowed. Did I really want to see these? Would there be anything there to see?

A heavy numbness filled my fingers. And I pushed the button. The screen lit up. A smiling picture of Keisha. Fake lashes, gorgeous eyes. Same oversized boyfriend shirt she'd been wearing that night.

Dylan's breath stuttered.

"Are you sure you're up for this?" I gazed sideways at him, not sure if I was ready for it. "It's only been a few days. We can always do it later."

Dylan shook his head. "No." He let out a long sigh and scooted so close our legs were nearly touching. "We need to see what's on there."

Mashing down the advance button, I flipped to the next picture and the next. Dylan and Keisha hanging out at the park before they came to Hunter's place. Smiling and in love. They did sort of look good together. Happy.

I clicked again. The Devil's Tree in the distance. Dylan must've been standing right outside Hunter's truck when he took it.

Nothing out of the ordinary. Just a tree, barren and tortured, but still a tree. I swallowed the strangling tightness around my throat and advanced to the next frame.

More pictures of the tree. In infrared. Black, twisted branches, reaching toward the moonlit sky.

Click.

Hunter. Smiling, handsome, sexy Hunter. Laughing. Warm. Alive. The tree behind him.

Click.

Hunter's back. A stream of pee disappearing against the tree trunk. I'd heard him going, but this was proof.

He'd done it. Gone and peed on that dang tree. Just like he said he'd do.

I swallowed and Dylan shifted on the bed beside me. I'd almost forgotten he was there.

Click.

Hunter's back. Still peeing.

I moved my finger to advance, but Dylan stopped me. "What's that?"

"What?" I looked closer.

"There." Dylan pointed to the branches, just beyond Hunter's head. It looked almost like a face appearing in the darkness.

"Probably just a shadow." My heart sped up, hammering against my ribs.

"Go to the next one."

Click.

Hunter wasn't peeing anymore. I could just see the shoulder of his T-shirt, but the image of the tree was clear.

Dylan gasped. So did I.

There was a face in the branches. In the tree. It was still there. Getting clearer.

Click. Click. Click.

The face grew clearer and clearer with every frame. A woman's weathered face. Others came into focus. Black and white. Men and women. Bodies emerged. Swinging from the tree like gruesome piñatas.

"Oh, God—" I swallowed and the camera went limp in my hands. "Is that—is that Old Joe?" He'd died in the ravine. It was just an accident. A terrible accident . . . unless the same truck that chased us off the road had chased him, too.

Dylan took the camera from me. Looked at the picture. He swallowed, licked his lips. "I think it is . . ." He advanced the frames, his face pale and sweaty. "It can't be—"

I stood up, ready to leave. I had to get away. Away from Dylan. Away from the camera. Away from the nightmare that had become my life.

My gaze flickered to the mirror, my heart leapt into my throat and strangled my scream: Hunter stood behind me. Bloody. Burned. Eyes pleading. His lips parted and his icy breath caressed my shoulder just before I bolted from the room.

Dylan bolted after me. The front door of our trailer slammed shut just seconds after I skittered out of the house —away from whatever nightmare I'd just seen in my bedroom mirror.

"Kaitlyn, wait!" Breathless, Dylan caught up to me near an old oak that shaded the front porch of our trailer.

I stood panting. Hunched over my skinny, bruised knees, I glanced up at him through a few stray blond hairs that had escaped my ponytail. "Did you see anything? In the mirror?"

Dylan squatted down in front of me, concern wrinkling his brows. "I didn't see anything but you did, didn't you? You looked terrified." He shook his head. "I should never have brought the camera here; that was a bad idea. Really stupid of me. I'm sorry."

My arms trembled. I couldn't help it. "Those pictures . . . they're scary." He hadn't seen Hunter in the mirror. Maybe Hunter hadn't been there. Maybe the pictures were all in my head, too. I must be going nuts. Maybe nuts like my mama when Daddy left us and she took up drinking. I took a deep breath. I couldn't go nuts like Mama. Not now. Not ever. No matter what. Who would take care of us then? *I'm just seeing things. It's only been a few days. I'm just seeing things.*

Dylan dragged his hands through his blond hair so it spiked up in a totally non-geeky way.

He held the camera out in front of him, took a deep, calming breath—probably to help both of us chill out—and scrolled through the photos. "There has to be a rational way to explain this."

Crap. He saw them, too. The pictures were real. "You think science can explain those?" I pushed the camera away from me. I didn't want to look at the faces haunting the branches of that tree. I wanted to destroy any memory of what had happened. Of what was happening.

Dylan pushed the power button off. "I'll put it away. But I still think there has to be an explanation for these images. And we're going to find it."

CHAPTER 3

I'd only ever been to church for a funeral. My gram's, when I was eight. What a mean old bat. While most kids' grandmas made cookies and lemonade, mine made moonshine and rolled tobacco. She even took me on weekly field trips to a drive-through liquor store. My mama wasn't much better.

I peeked into Mama's bedroom, which was only slightly larger than mine. Avoiding her bedroom mirror, which I'd been doing since I thought I'd seen Hunter lurking in mine, I stepped into her room. She was passed out on her double-sized mattress with a large brown stain and no sheets. The mess in her room was almost as awful as the thought of Keisha and Hunter somehow being ghosts. I shuddered and picked up a pair of her dirty jeans. I hadn't done any laundry since the accident. I guess I wouldn't get much slack. It had to be done and Mama was in no shape to do it.

A few years ago I might've worried she was dead, but now I knew what passed-out drunk looked like—and she was it. Sound asleep, she was still in the jeans and T-shirt she'd worn when a neighbor brought her to see me in the hospital the night of the accident. An empty bottle of whiskey was rolled up next to her. Maybe that had caused the stain. But probably not. It wasn't like Mama to waste any booze.

She wasn't so bad before Daddy left. Back then she'd only have a couple drinks with him at night. She'd been okay. She'd even come to parent orientation when I started middle school. But that'd all changed three years ago when Daddy left us.

I sighed, pulled a blanket off the floor, and held it to my nose. It smelled faintly of cigarette smoke and strongly of whiskey. I tossed it into the unused clothes hamper, then pulled another blanket from Mama's tiny closet. I smelled that one: laundry detergent and lavender. Good, clean smells. I put the blanket over her and tucked it under her chin. She made a small noise and her lips flickered into a smile.

My heart lurched. I never saw Mama smile anymore. I hadn't realized how much I'd missed it. I shook my head. It irked me she couldn't even get it together for Hunter and Keisha's funerals. She'd known Keisha since we were in kindergarten, and Hunter since middle school. She'd taken me and Keisha to the park when we were younger, and chaperoned my first date with Hunter. I half-smiled at the memory. We'd had some fun times. Now all she did was go and collect welfare; that was about the only thing she was good for anymore.

After locking up the trailer, I trudged the quarter mile to St. Phillip's alone. My little black dress was riding up my thighs and pissing me off with every step. At least I had a decent pair of black flats since my heels were ruined when we went to see that damned tree. Ruined right along with everything else in my life that night. I sighed. Without Hunter, I didn't have a best friend. I didn't have an escape plan from this town. And, more urgently, I didn't have a ride. I'd flat-out refused to go with Dylan. Despite having to walk everywhere in the dang summer heat without A/C, it didn't bother me much. I wasn't really up to getting into another car anytime soon anyhow.

Leaves rustled and a bird chirped overhead as I rounded the corner to Third Street. Hunter didn't go to church. Keisha was Baptist. How the funerals had come to be in our neighborhood Catholic church was a mystery to me. Some rich folks from the church had probably offered to pay for the funerals.

The church parking lot was already full, like the entire town had decided to come and say their goodbyes. Likely most of them just wanted to say they were part of the whole horrific thing. There wasn't much excitement in Harland; the accident had been something. I shivered, Hunter's burned and bloody face still fresh in my mind.

My hands trembled when I reached the door, my heart screaming at me not to go in. I told my heart to shut up, then opened the glass front door and went inside to a press of bodies and the smell of perfume and sweat and tears. I gagged and my world went all woozy.

I steadied myself on a table covered with church flyers. All of the chatter buzzed like a fly around my brain and I swallowed my partially digested Jimmy Dean breakfast biscuit back down. That's when I made the mistake of peering into the sanctuary.

Two coffins. Hunter's and Keisha's. Both wood. Both closed. They had to be closed. From what I'd heard, the bodies were so badly burned they'd had a hard time identifying them.

The room got blurry and I felt myself dropping.

Someone reached in and grabbed me, just before I hit

the floor. Dylan. I smelled him before I saw him. Abercrombie. I loved that scent. Just not on him.

I wanted to push away that smell. Push away those arms, the same arms that had held me back from the truck that awful night. But he wasn't letting go. Maybe I really didn't want him to. "Hey, take it easy. I've got you." Dylan sat me in a nearby chair. My vision twisted and I gulped down air, trying not to throw up.

"Is she alright?" A Hispanic man in black robes with a white collar came over to us, concern clear on his face.

"I'm fine." I answered before Dylan could. I made my eyes focus. "It's just a lot to take in, is all."

Dylan frowned and glanced over to where his mama, with her caked-on mascara and fake concern, hovered near Hunter's and Keisha's parents. Keisha's folks, her aunt and uncle, a handful of cousins, and a few friends from school were the only dark faces in a sea of white. Most people acted like color didn't matter anymore—at least on the surface. It had never mattered a hill of beans to me. But the truth was we still had black churches and white churches in Harland. And St. Phillip's was definitely a white one.

Still, I was glad they were here. They were good people, Keisha's mom and dad. Keisha's daddy was the first successful black baker our town had ever seen. Didn't matter what color he was, people loved his cookies and cakes and bread. His love for baking and good food brought people together. He had respect. But more than anything, I loved them because they'd always been kind to me. They had me over every holiday. They made sure I had good meals and got Christmas gifts. And, of course, Keisha's daddy helped me out when Mama didn't remember my birthday. Every year I had a nice birthday cake.

Hunter's mama cackled, making Keisha's parents give her uncomfortable smiles. That woman was a known gossip; she could talk a raccoon right out of a tree if she wanted. Gossip or not, at least she was here. That was better than I could say for Dylan's daddy or my mama. Dylan's daddy might have been the primary donor for the funerals, but if he was, I knew his charity wasn't 'cause he cared. All he wanted was to look good to folks in town—to appear charitable. It was definitely better that Mr. Anderson wasn't here. He wasn't a nice man.

Keisha never went over to Dylan's house. She'd said his daddy was the most racist man she'd ever met. And that was saying something—since the black folks in town generally lived on one side of the train tracks and the whites lived on the other. The only place we overlapped was in the trailer park where I lived. There, color didn't matter. Life in the trailer park was more about survival than race. God only knew how Dylan's parents reacted when they'd found out he was dating Keisha. They were probably glad she was dead.

I sucked back a sob. It was so unfair. All of it. They should be alive. We should all be graduating together next year.

"I'm Father Eduardo Alvarez." The priest's voice pulled me from my thoughts. He extended his hand to Dylan, then to me. He glanced at the fresh scabs and yellowing bruises on my knees and face, and at Dylan's black eye. He had to know who we were. Our last year's high school pictures were plastered all over the newspaper: the living and the dead.

Dylan nodded and said something I didn't catch.

Father Alvarez smiled. "I'll be officiating the funerals for Hunter and Keisha."

A sort of sick feeling washed over me and I leaned

forward, head over my knees, and tried not to puke. Oh. My. Gosh. Hunter's funeral. Keisha's. My pulse raced and sweat broke out all over my face.

Robed all in black, Father Alvarez squatted in front of me and put his hand on my shoulder. "God is infinitely merciful. They are at peace."

I looked up at him then, real quick. Was he kidding or did he really believe that? His eyes were serious. And he wasn't that old. Younger than I'd imagine a priest to be. Probably only in his forties. "How do you know?"

Dylan stiffened beside me. A silent warning not to mention the images we'd seen on his camera.

"God keeps all created things in existence." The father smiled kindly.

"Hunter didn't go to church," I said before I could stop myself. I wished he had. I wished I had. Maybe I'd feel less frightened about where Hunter and Keisha were now if I'd spent time in church. Maybe I'd feel less trapped in this situation. Shoot, I didn't know what happened after we died. Did we go to heaven or hell? Was God even real? Or did we just fade away into nothingness? I shivered. I didn't want that. There had to be more to life than just drifting off and being gone. Besides, I know what I saw in those pictures and in the mirror. Somehow Hunter was still here. Somehow his spirit had survived. Unless my head was playing tricks with me.

"A just man—or woman—merits for himself through each good work an increase of sanctifying grace, eternal life, and heavenly glory. I'm sure your friends were just. God knew Hunter's heart—even if Hunter didn't go to church."

A tear slid down my cheek, and I fought to hold back the deluge. I hoped Father Alvarez was right. I hoped God was real. And I hoped He had mercy on Hunter and

Keisha and had taken them both right on up to the pearly gates where color and income didn't matter. I hoped they weren't really stuck here. Being alive here was bad enough.

A bell tolled overhead. "The service is about to start. I have two rows reserved for family and close friends. Please, let me see you to your seats."

Dylan gently took my arm and helped me to my feet. We followed Father Alvarez into the sanctuary and took our seats in the front row, a massive crucifix looming above the altar not five feet from us.

Keisha's mama and daddy were sitting close. Her mama was crying hard. Her daddy gave me a sad smile, then wrapped his arm around Keisha's mama. Hunter's mama dabbed at the smeared mascara on her face, but her eyes were dry. Likely as not she was drunk. That's one thing me and Hunter had in common. Our mamas liked the booze, even if his was able to function when mine was passed out drunk.

I couldn't stop staring at Hunter's coffin. Imagining him in there all burned and charred and crispy. A ruined shell. He'd always been so damned sexy. Sexy and kind and young. Way too young to be dead.

The father was saying something. I could barely focus on his words, but I tried to listen to his prayer.

"Lord our God, You are always faithful and quick to show mercy. Keisha and Hunter were suddenly taken from us. Come swiftly to their aid, have mercy on them, and comfort their families and friends by the power and protection of the cross. We ask this through Christ our Lord. Amen."

The word *Amen* echoed through the room, clinging to the air. It was a nice prayer, but all I could do was think that Keisha and Hunter were gone.

Gone.

Forever.

I couldn't stand that Hunter wasn't ever going to pick me up again and take me out to Mojo's. I couldn't stand that I'd never feel his soft lips on mine. I couldn't stand that I wouldn't have him to help me survive in this little town with an alcoholic mother who relied on me to pay the bills because she was too drunk to work. Hunter and I'd had an escape plan. We were supposed to move away from this town, move away from our parents, move away from all the ass-backwards people around us. But now, Hunter was gone and my plans along with him.

Tears spilled down my face, and my body shook so hard I felt like my ribs might bust out through my chest.

Dylan was crying too, but I barely paid him any mind. He'd only been with Keisha for a few months. Hunter'd been my life.

Dylan handed me a box of tissues, then put his arm around me. It was warm and comforting. I hadn't expected that. It made me cry harder. I didn't want to lean on Dylan. I wanted to hate him for taking us to that damned tree. I wanted to hate him for surviving. Why did he live and Hunter die? But it didn't matter right then. I just laid my head on Dylan's shoulder and cried and cried and cried.

That's when I heard the scream.

It wasn't just a regular I-saw-a-bug scream. It was a full-throated, I'm-gonna-kill-you wail. One that sent shivers to my toes, made the lights go out, and caused the whole room to fall quiet.

Through the darkness, candle flames flickering atop cross-adorned pillars, I could just make her out. Standing about three feet in front of the coffins was Keisha. Burned, but ghostly pale. And madder than hell. "Don't you touch my Dylan," she howled at me.

I screamed then and lunged to my feet. Tripping over Dylan, I shot out of the pew and headed for the exit.

"Kaitlyn, stop." Oh. My God. It was Hunter's voice.

Spinning around, I found Dylan behind me, eyes wide with fright. People were up and talking. Some were crying. People were looking around, calling for someone to check the circuit breakers.

Through the dim light, not too far from the coffins, I saw him. Tall and burned and bloody. Hunter. My Hunter.

"Don't you tell her to stop, Hunter McMaster. She was laying her head on my man. You should be pissed, too. You even told me you thought he liked her." Keisha had her hands on her hips and a scowl on her face. I knew that look. The one she reserved for people who'd really ticked her off—like the time I'd given her new Barbie a haircut. I remember truly wanting to give that doll a haircut because it was fun, but I also remember being jealous that Keisha had a new Barbie and all I had was a hand-me-down knockoff, whose head and arms kept falling off.

"None of that matters now." Hunter frowned at Keisha then looked back at me. "Help us, Kaitlyn. You have to help us."

Dylan pushed open the door into the hazy summer sun and grabbed my hand. Somewhere behind us, Keisha screamed again, and we ran out into the light.

Now I knew for certain that Father Alvarez's prayer had fallen flat. God hadn't had mercy on them, and Keisha and Hunter sure as hell were not in heaven.

CHAPTER 4

I ROLLED OVER IN BED, THE COVERS TANGLING AROUND my legs, determined not to leave my room again today. I hadn't been out for food since the funeral yesterday—only to pee twice and to make sure Mama ate breakfast. Thankfully my manager at the Food Mart had given me an extra week off. We needed the money, but I couldn't bring myself to face the folks in town. Lord knows they'd all be in there to check on me and get the latest gossip.

Despite being three sheets gone, Mama even tried to bring me lunch this afternoon. I'd heard the sheriff out there talking to her. Telling her to take care of me. Telling her that I wasn't right in the head after such a traumatic accident—having been there when my friends died and all. I suppose Mama making lunch for me was her way of trying. But she was gone now. She'd stood outside my room and said something about going out to get the welfare check and then to the store—probably for more booze.

I lay back on my skinny, springy mattress, pulled my quilt up to my chin, and prayed I didn't get another visit from Keisha or Hunter. This was my space. My little place in the world—even if it only had two tiny windows and faded wallpaper with little yellow buds. Paper from a happier time when Mama'd tried to cover up the ratty, mildewed paneling underneath. From a time when she still cared.

My room could barely hold a single bed, a skinny, battered chest of drawers, and an old schoolhouse desk tucked into the corner of the room. A desk too small for any studying, barely big enough for a lamp and my plastic jewelry. I didn't care if it wasn't much. It was mine. And I didn't need ghosts taking it away from me.

Darkness was beginning to peek through the gap in my blinds and I figured maybe it was time I got out of bed and got some dinner. That's when someone started banging on the front door. Not a quiet bang, but a really annoying, I'm-not-leaving-until-you-answer-type bang.

I pulled the covers over my head and tried to ignore it.

The banging just got louder.

They'd get bored and go away eventually, right?

It stopped and I sighed.

Then someone banged even louder right on my bedroom window and I nearly fell outta bed.

"Come on, Kaitlyn, I know you're in there." It was Dylan. "When I called, your mom told me you won't come out of your room. So I'm here to get you out."

I scowled and pulled the covers over my head.

He banged again. "Open up or I'll just keep knocking until your mom gets home and lets me in."

At three o'clock in the morning when Curtis's Bar closed? Right. With a growl, I tossed back the covers, walked two feet to my window, yanked open my flimsy plastic blinds, and threw open my window. "What do you want?" I yelled even though he was a foot in front of me, not giving a crap who saw me in my sweatpants and faded Texas A&M shirt, the one my dad had brought me the Christmas before he left.

Dylan held up a plastic shopping bag. "We have to deal with this, Kaitlyn. They won't just go away on their own."

"What on God's good earth have you got in there?" Pictures from the one-hour photo lab? A ghost-hunting kit? I could barely begin to imagine.

"Something that's going to help us find out exactly what's going on with Keisha and Hunter. Now open up."

Three minutes later Dylan was in my postage-stamp-sized room. In all the years I'd known him, he'd never been in our trailer, let alone my bedroom, until the accident. Hunter was the only guy other than my dad who'd been in here. I had a little pang of guilt. Did Hunter really think Dylan liked me the way Keisha'd said? Like, really liked me? No way. But it might explain why she'd started getting all pissy with me lately. Maybe she thought Dylan liked me —even if it was crazy.

I perched on the desk next to the window, chewed my nails, and eyed the plastic bag Dylan held in front of him.

"No one else at church may have seen what we did. But I know what I saw, Kaitlyn. And we're going to find out exactly what's happening with Keisha and Hunter." He gave me a crooked grin, pulled a box out of the bag, and tossed it on my bed.

"What's that?" I asked without really looking at it.

"A Ouija board." He sat on my bed, tore off the clear wrapping, and opened the lid. "Before we even saw what we did at the funeral, you got me thinking about the pictures." He adjusted the glasses on the bridge of his nose. "I don't know how or why we saw them in the photos. I don't know how or why we saw what we did at the funeral. But I heard them, Kaitlyn. I saw them. I saw

Keisha and Hunter." He looked straight at me then. "And so did you."

I shook my head, wishing I had left Dylan outside to pound on my window instead of having him inside, sitting on my bed, where he could pound on my brain.

"So, I did some research." He pulled a little off-white pointer thingy out of the box and set it on my bed.

"Research, huh? That's what got us in this mess to begin with, Dylan Anderson." Dylan and his curiosity about that cursed tree. I wasn't sure if I really wanted to know where this was going.

"Look, if the photos were prints, I'd say someone had played a mean trick on us. But they weren't. And it's my camera. I've had it with me since I left the hospital, and the photos haven't even been downloaded yet. So, there's no way someone could have manipulated the images."

"So?" I was getting impatient now. It wasn't just about the camera or the pictures. I'd seen Hunter in the mirror and we'd both seen him and Keisha at the funeral.

"So, between that evidence and the fact we both saw and heard Keisha and Hunter, but no one else did, it appears we're being haunted." He pulled an antique-looking game board from the box and opened it up.

The board was coffee-stain brown, like some old photos I'd seen in my gram's house when I was little. It had the alphabet and numbers across the center, all in white. Up in the left corner was the picture of a sun, and beneath it, the word *yes*. Up in the right corner was a moon, and beneath it, the word *no*. At the top, surrounded in black, was the word *Ouija*. And at the bottom was one word: *goodbye*.

A strange sensation crept over me, like flies' wings beating against my bare skin. Arms crossed over my chest, I tried to ignore the board. It was just a game. A stupid game. Still, looking at it gave me the willies. "Well, that's just great, Dylan. I'm so glad you've come to the conclusion that we saw ghosts. Now can we just say goodbye and get on with our lives? Maybe that was their grand finale. Maybe they were making their last show at the funeral, and they're all done and now they're gone. They have to be because starting next week I have to go back to work." Of course, I didn't believe a word of what I'd just said— except the work part. I didn't think I'd ever say goodbye to Hunter. Not really. Not in my heart. But, man, becoming a ghost hunter was *not* on my to-do list.

He set the board down on his lap and looked at me. "Work? You just went to a funeral. Won't they give you more time off?"

"Sure they will, but we can't afford it." I gestured to our dingy trailer. "And Mama's not likely to get a job anytime soon."

"I can give you some money." Dylan pulled out his leather wallet.

"Are you freakin' kidding me?" I snapped. "Don't be an asshole." I wouldn't take handouts. Not now. Not ever. I would not be like my mother.

He slowly stuffed his wallet back in his pocket. "I'm sorry, Kaitlyn. I was just"

"I know. You're just trying to help." I sighed bitterly. Everyone tried to help after Daddy left, but that didn't stop Mama from drinking. Actually, she drank up all that charity in vodka and whiskey and wine. So much for trying to help me go to college. If I ever escaped this godforsaken town, I'd have to do it on my own. But with Mama in such bad shape and Hunter dead, I doubted that'd ever happen. Not unless I came up with a new plan and managed to save more than Mama spent on drinks.

Dylan held up the little plastic pointer thing that he'd

taken from the box and pulled me out of my stupor. "We can use the Ouija board to figure out if they're still here."

I shook my head. I wanted no part of this. I didn't want Hunter dead, but I didn't want to go calling him back from the grave either.

"Come on, Kaitlyn." Dylan set the plastic pointer down and gave me desperate, puppy-dog eyes. Eyes that made me think of Hunter when he was trying to get me to do something I swore I wouldn't do. "You heard Hunt."

"His name's Hunter. Ya know, with an *-er*." Sometimes I hated being bitchy, but there's no way I was going to go along with this if I had to listen to Dylan calling Hunter "Hunt." It'd been my pet peeve for years, but Hunter hadn't given a crap. He'd laugh and tell me it was Dylan's nickname for him. Yeah, right. He didn't go around calling Dylan "Dill" or something. The whole thing was so stupid. Hunt. It made Hunter sound like some sort of ketchup or tomato sauce. Something cheap. Which he wasn't.

Dylan's puppy-dog eyes transformed into a glare. "Hunt-er," he said each syllable for emphasis through gritted teeth, "said he needs help. Are you really going to turn your back on him now?"

Ouch. That hurt. And I knew Dylan meant it too. Damn him. "Of course I heard Hunter, but what am I supposed to do about it? Maybe that was their final show and they're gone now that their bodies have been laid to rest."

Dylan picked up the pointer and set it on the Ouija board. "Then humor me. We'll try to contact them through the Ouija board. If they don't answer, then I'll go along with you. They're gone. I'd be okay with that. If they're at peace, then we have nothing to worry about. But if they do answer, then we need to find out why they're here and how we can help them."

Suddenly I just felt so exhausted. Dylan was as stubborn as Hunter. Maybe there was actually something to that friendship. I sat on the bed, the Ouija board between us. "Fine. Let's get this over with. Just tell me what I have to do."

———

TWO CANDLES GLOWED in the soft pink light of dusk, one on my tiny desk, the other on my chest of drawers. Dylan had bought them with the game board, thinking it would help set the mood for trying to contact Keisha and Hunter if we turned off all the lights and just used candles. I'd snorted at him, saying he'd watched too many horror movies, but had gone along with it. The sooner this was over, the sooner we could try to get on with our shattered lives.

With the board set up on my bedroom floor, Dylan lightly placed his fingers on the pointer and looked at me. "This," he said, "is called a planchette. It will help us contact the other side. No matter what, don't move the planchette. If they're still here, they'll move it on their own."

Of course, I wouldn't move it. What point would that make? I placed my fingers on the pointer thingy and silently prayed no one would answer our call.

"Do you want me to ask the questions or do you want to?"

"You do it," I said, nearly pulling my fingers off the pointer. "This is all you, buddy."

"Keep your fingers on it. You've got to put your energy into it if it's going to work," Dylan growled.

I kept my fingers lightly on the plastic. "If they're still here, they won't need my energy." Hunter hadn't needed it to scare me half to death in my bedroom mirror, and he and Keisha hadn't needed it to show up and blow out the lights in church. "Get on with it, Dylan. It's getting dark out." And I definitely didn't want to be doing this at night. Doing it at dusk was creepy enough.

He took a deep breath, then focused on the board. "I'm calling out to the spirits of Keisha Richards and Hunter McMaster. If you're still here, Kaitlyn and I want to talk with you."

We sat there stiffly, only the buzz of silence filling our ears.

My arms began to ache and I wiggled uncomfortably, but a sharp look from Dylan made me stop moving.

"Keisha and Hunter," he called. "If you're here, please use this board to talk to us. We want to help you."

More silence.

The kind of silence that seems so hungry it'll eat you up completely if you let it.

I was about ready to pull my hands off the pointer when I noticed my breath in the air. The humming window unit in the next room barely made a dent in this muggy summer heat that crept inside the trailer, but with each exhale my breath came out in icy white puffs and my lips tingled with cold. Gooseflesh prickled up and down my arms, and a little feeling inside of me, a little voice that told me something bad was about to happen, started nagging at me. That's when the pointer started to move. Not a big move at first, just a little twitch.

"Are you doing that?" I asked, fear clutching my throat.

Dylan shook his head, the pale glow of candlelight reflecting off his glasses. "No," he whispered. "Keisha? Is that you?"

The pointer lurched upward, past the alphabet, toward the moon in the upper right-hand corner of the board.

It stopped on the word *no*.

Shivers shot over my spine, but not from the cold. I knew I wasn't moving it, and if Dylan had been, Keisha would be the person he'd want to talk to most – so I didn't think he was moving it either.

"If it's not Keisha, then who is this?" His voice was husky, nearly breaking with emotion.

The planchette twitched, then slowly began circling the letters.

"Who is this?" Dylan asked again, more calmly.

The planchette began weaving over the letters before finally stopping on the H. After that it spelled more quickly, stopping on each letter in turn: H – U – N – T – E – R.

Tears filled my eyes. "Hunter?" My voice cracked. "How do we know it's really you?"

The pointer shot over toward me, nearly leaping off the board. I scooted back a few inches, but kept my fingers on the planchette. "Please, tell me how I know it's really you?"

The pointer slowly moved back up to the letters and began spelling out words:

Y – O – U. It circled back toward me, then went back to the alphabet. D – R – E – A – M. The planchette hovered in the center of the board for a second, then continued: T – O. B – E. A. It came to me one last time before spelling out the final word: N – U – R – S – E.

Oh. My. God. I'd never told anyone that. Not my counselor at school. Not Keisha when we'd been besties. Not Mama. No one except Hunter knew that. It had to be him.

I don't know when I started crying, but tears streamed down my cheeks. "It's you . . . it's really you. Oh, I'm so sorry, Hunter. I'm so, so sorry. We tried to get you out. Me and Dylan tried to get you and Keisha both out of the car, but it exploded." I gasped back a sob. "I miss you so damned much."

The planchette went crazy, zipping from me to Dylan, then back to the alphabet on the board. It frantically spelled out a message: "GO BACK TO THE TREE OR WE WILL BE TRAPPED. FOREVER."

CHAPTER 5

"There's no way in hell I'm going back to that tree." I yanked my hands off the pointer and scooched back against my bed.

"You can't just end a session, Kaitlyn. It says so in the directions," Dylan hissed, focusing back on the board. "Spirits of Hunter and Keisha and anyone else who is here, please go in peace until we speak again." Dylan guided the planchette to *goodbye*, then let it go.

A pained, worried look gripping his face, he packed everything back in the box, and then leaned his head against the dingy wall.

I shoved the Ouija board into a cobwebbed corner under the desk with my toe, vowing I'd never touch that thing again. Even if it was just a game, it was totally creepy.

"Did you move the planchette?" He looked at me, his eyes deadly serious.

"Do I look like I moved it?" I hopped up on my bed and pulled my knees under my chin, hoping nothing would jump out and grab me from the slim seam of blackness beneath my box springs.

Dylan twisted his class ring round and round his finger, never taking his eyes off me. "No," he said. "You don't."

"Did you?" I peeked up at him, half-hoping he'd pushed it, but I knew Dylan well enough to trust he wouldn't have.

"Of course not." He sat beside me and rubbed his chin. "I don't have an explanation, but I know what I saw at the funeral. I know their spirits are here. But if that was really him . . . then Hunter and Keisha are trapped in that tree. And if they're trapped, then we have to do something to help. We can't just leave them there."

"What do you want us to do? The cops don't believe a damned thing we told them about the black truck." No tire tracks. No tread marks. No evidence, they'd said. They said we were making it up based on the town's stories. But they sure as heck seemed scared of something to me, like they couldn't close the case fast enough. "You want to take on an investigation ourselves? Go and shoot more pictures? We'll get chased by the same damn truck and we could get killed this time!" My voice rose with every word. We were all supposed to graduate from high school next year. Now two of us were dead.

"No." He pointed to the Ouija board. "I say we take that with us and find out who or what is keeping them trapped."

"Same thing."

"No. It's not. No camera and no peeing—"

"Oh, what? Now it's Hunter's fault?"

"No. Kaitlyn, stop. Hunt—Hunt*er*—was my best friend. He was who he was. I'm just saying, we'll do things differently this time. We'll be quiet. Respectful. We'll find answers."

Shivers crawled all over me like a mound of fire ants set loose at a picnic. That was so not a good idea. "Is this the same Dylan who wouldn't go off-roading with Hunter last summer because it was too dangerous?"

Dylan frowned. "That was different. And we'll do more research first. Not just the Google searches I did about accidents out there. We'll see what we can find about someone living—or dying—near that tree."

"We already know about Old Joe. The whole town does." My voice trembled and hitched itself up a notch. I couldn't shake the image of him out of my mind. Old Joe in that photo. Hanging from that tree. Flannel shirt, dirty beard, bloated corpse. That dang truck must have driven him off the road and into the ravine. It killed him just like it killed Hunter and Keisha. I bounced my knees up and down, making my bed squeak.

"But there are stories of other accidents out there. Other people have died. You know we've heard whispers about it all our lives. What we need to do is to really dig into the history of the area. We need to do more research." Dylan laid a hand across my legs to stop the bouncing, and a little jolt of hormones went racing through me. Oh, no. That was not okay. No one touched my knees but Hunter. No one made my hormones go racing like that except him either. I pulled away from Dylan, wrapping my old quilt tightly around me. Could Keisha have been right? Did Dylan want more from me now than I could give?

"It's okay, Kaitlyn. We'll go together. It might give us important information. So at least we'll know what we're up against."

"You're crazy," I said, knowing I was getting sucked into a plan I wanted no part of.

Dylan's iPhone buzzed. He glanced at the screen, which wasn't cracked like mine. Granted, his was brand-new and mine was a hand-me-down from Mama's friend at the welfare office.

"It's my dad," he groaned and tapped the ignore button. "I'd better go. But meet me at my house tomorrow morning at ten o'clock—sharp."

"Your house?" Aside from the Devil's Tree, the last place I wanted to go was Dylan's house. Especially not if his mama or daddy were there. They'd like my trailer upbringing just about as much as they'd liked the color of Keisha's skin.

"Just meet me there." Dylan sighed, like this wasn't the first time he'd had to convince someone to come to his house.

"I guess," I said, far from convinced I'd even leave my room tomorrow.

———

MY EYES SHOT open and I stared at the bloodred numbers on my alarm clock: 2:03 a.m. I didn't even remember falling asleep. The last time I'd checked it was just past nine. Sweat plastered my T-shirt to my body and I wiped damp hair out of my face. Everything was quiet except for the faint hum of the window unit that pumped air into our living room, barely snaking its way under my door.

I kicked my quilt to the end of the bed and settled back, pulling the sheet to my chin. I didn't like to sleep without covers—no matter how hot it was. Something about being all wrapped up and cocoon-like was comforting, safe. But the darkened silence of the room pressed in on me, like a covering of black wool over my eyes and ears. Not even moonlight seemed to make its way through my too-thin curtains. I closed my eyes, trying to shut out the eerie silence of my room, and hoped I could go back to sleep.

A jiggling, rustling sort of sound made my eyes snap back open.

Sheet pulled tight, I sat up. Peeking over the edge of my bed, I stared at the Ouija board box still tucked under my desk, just beneath my plaid curtained window. Crap. Dylan forgot to take it with him. Or maybe he'd left it on purpose so I'd have to go to his house to give it back.

Another rustling sound.

I swear it was coming from the box.

Oh, Lord, I didn't want to see Hunter or Keisha again. Not dead, anyway. And not in the middle of the night.

Rustle. Rustle. Rustle.

Dammit, Dylan. Why'd you have to go and bring a Ouija board into my bedroom?

Shoving my fear aside, I threw back my sheet and stepped toward the box.

Rustle. Rustle. Rustle.

Oh. My. Gosh. It moved. My heart rate sped up in time with the jiggling box.

There was no way I could go back to sleep with that thing in my room. I had to get it out of here. And the quicker, the better.

Shoving the curtains out of my way, I unlatched the window, opened it, and popped out the screen. Warm, muggy air slammed into me, plastering my hair to my face.

I reached over and grabbed the Ouija board, ready to hurl it as far away from my window as possible.

That's when a huge tree roach scurried out of the box and scuttled across my bare foot. I screamed and dropped it so the lid popped off.

It's not like I wasn't used to seeing roaches. In this part of Texas we had tons of them. Great big flying ones. The kind that liked to dive-bomb your head in parking lots at night on account of the big, blazing streetlights. I never quite understood why roaches did that, but it gave me the willies. Still, I sure as heck wasn't used to seeing them in my bedroom. Mama at least had the sense to buy roach traps and bombs when we needed them. Ugh. I'd buy more when I was back to work at the Food Mart.

Then I laughed. Me. Afraid of a dumb, freakin' roach. I watched it skitter up the wall and out my window. Good riddance. I kicked the Ouija board box across my room and stubbed my toe. "Ouch. Stupid game." At least it was a roach and not some ghost. I sighed and closed the window. Dylan could come and get his Ouija board tomorrow—after he spent some alone time at home with his laptop. Seriously, only Mensa-boy Dylan would think research could give you anti-ghost super powers.

I turned back toward bed and stopped dead. Chilly air wrapped itself around me and my breath came out in billowy white puffs. Goose bumps crawled over my skin, and I shivered. That's when I saw her. Through the waiting darkness of my room.

Keisha.

Sitting on my bed, she fixed her angry eyes on mine. "I know you, Kaitlyn Karly. I know who you are. I know what you're like. And I may be dead, but I can still hurt you," she hissed. "You stay away from Dylan. Or I'll never leave you alone."

———

I'D BEEN SITTING outside of St. Phillip's Catholic Church, Father Alvarez's church, since 3:00 a.m. The minute Keisha spoke, I bolted out of my room, and I wasn't sure I'd ever go back. It wasn't like her. Not the Keisha I'd known. My Keisha had been friendly and confident and happy. That is, until she got all boy crazy over Dylan. Still, she had never been mean. This Keisha was pissed as hell at me and I didn't know why. I'd never try to take her man – ever. That was crazy. I loved Keisha. Something was seriously wrong. Maybe that's what dying did to her . . . went and made her bat-ass crazy.

At first I'd wandered, chilled in the T-shirt and jeans I'd grabbed from the laundry line after busting out my front door, but then I came up on the church and it seemed like the best place to hide from ghosts. I'd been here since. Waiting. Hoping. Praying. Not that praying was something I'd ever really done. The last time I'd prayed was when Daddy left. But he hadn't come back and I'd given up on the idea of a God who cared.

I never thought I'd go into a church again. Not after the funeral. Not ever. But if anyone would know how to deal with spirits, it would be a Catholic priest, right? Sooner or later, Father Alvarez would show up. I preferred sooner.

I wasn't much for going to church. And when I did go, I usually dressed up. I guess God would have to forgive me looking scruffy. I clutched the hunter-green messenger bag Hunter'd given me last Christmas, which I'd snagged from my porch after changing out of my PJs in the early morning darkness. The bag had been sitting there, next to my sneakers, making me think of Hunter. It was way more dude-like than anything I'd ever used before, but he'd said it'd be good for me to have something "utilitarian" that also had a color that bore his name. I'd scoffed about it at the time and told him he shouldn't have wasted his money. Now, I was glad I had the bag not only could I fit a lot of my crap inside, but it also gave me a way to keep a little piece of Hunter right beside me.

A dark blue Chevy pulled up, which was now the only car in the parking lot. There weren't many churchgoers at

8:30 on a Friday morning. I sighed and stretched out my stiff legs. Sitting on the concrete entryway for over five hours had made my still-bruised butt hurt even more.

Father Alvarez's booted feet and blue jean–clad legs emerged first. He stood up, then shut his car door with a thud, revealing a different man than I'd seen at the funeral. Not only was he wearing cowboy boots and jeans, but also an Astros T-shirt with no robes in sight. Really? A baseball-loving cowboy Catholic priest. Huh. Maybe I wasn't so underdressed after all.

And maybe our town was actually starting to change. I didn't think we'd had a Hispanic priest in town before. At least not that I knew of. It reminded me of a time Daddy'd said that when he was a boy no one would've gone to Keisha's daddy's bakery on account of him being black. I'd never understood that. Keisha's daddy was the best baker around and what on God's good earth did skin color have to do with his baking?

But Daddy said things were changing, and that now it didn't matter to most people what color their baker or barber or dentist was so long as he was good at what he did. I was only around thirteen when he said that, but I remember thinking it was all very strange. Why would someone judge someone else because of their color? It made no sense at all. I sure as hell never cared about the color of Keisha's skin. Black or white, pink or purple. Keisha was Keisha. I guess that's how Dylan saw it, too, even if his daddy didn't.

Father Alvarez saw me as soon as he shut the car door, his gaze flittering around the parking lot, then back to me. "Kaitlyn. Are you okay?"

With two-day-old smudged makeup, no sleep, and lingering bruises, I'm sure I looked anything but okay. And I felt like crap. But I wasn't going to say all that. Now that he was here, I wasn't entirely sure how to even mention seeing ghosts. No one at the funeral had seemed to see anything but the lights go out and me and Dylan running like lunatics from the church. For all I knew, they thought I was crazier than a cat who'd drunk a bucket of moonshine. So, I shrugged.

"Long night?"

"You could say that." I climbed stiffly to my feet.

Silently, he unlocked the double glass front doors and led me inside.

I stopped in the doorway to his office, wondering if Keisha and Hunter would appear here again on church land now that their bodies were buried by a priest in hallowed ground. I wasn't one to give much thought to superstition before the accident. Between work and school, I hadn't had time for it—or much of anything else. Still, they'd showed up in my room since they were buried. So, I guessed they could show up just about anywhere.

Father Alvarez put his things beside his desk and looked up at me still lurking in his doorway. "Please, come in."

I didn't move an inch.

"There's nothing here that will hurt you, Kaitlyn."

I crossed my arms over my chest and shoved back a shudder. Maybe. Maybe not.

He opened his hands to me, his smile warm. "I promise." He gestured to the chairs in front of his desk. "Please. Sit down. I'll get you some tea."

"Coffee. Black," I barked without meaning to. I needed the caffeine if I was going to make it through the day. "Please," I added lamely. "I'm more of a coffee girl." Hunter used to treat me to a Starbucks every Sunday afternoon. I sure was gonna miss that quiet time with him. The time we dreamed about our lives together after high school. Our lives after getting out of this town.

The father nodded and went into an adjoining room I assumed was the kitchen.

Before I could read the copy of the Apostles' Creed hanging on Father Alvarez's wall, he was back. He set down a steaming mug in front of me, then held a cup to his lips. He took a sip, eyes never leaving my face.

I picked up my cup and stared into the dark liquid, letting the comforting warmth of the mug seep into my fingers.

"So," he asked, setting down his mug, "you're having trouble sleeping?"

"Yeah." How lame. I squeezed my cup hard, then took a sip. My thoughts and fears twisted together, making everything I'd seen and heard seem totally crazy. Would Father Alvarez believe me? Would he call Mama? Social services? The police? I needed to tell him, but how?

"What happened to you and Dylan and your friends was a terrible tragedy. I know the funeral was extremely difficult for you both. It's normal to grieve and feel angry and uncomfortable. Pope Benedict XVI once said, 'The ways of the Lord are not comfortable, but we were not created for comfort, but for greatness, for good.'"

Was that supposed to make me feel better? There was hardly anything great or good about the deaths of Hunter or Keisha or my miserable life. Teeth clenched so tight so I wouldn't say something I'd regret, I felt my jaws ache. Maybe I'd made a big mistake coming here. Telling people my feelings and asking for prayer just wasn't me. Not even after Daddy left. But what choice did I have if I wanted help? Who else could I turn to?

"But I sense there's something you're not telling me. Something that's bothering you." He opened his hands on the desk – as if welcoming me in. "That's what I'm here for. You can talk to me."

"Yeah" I let the word out with a breath, hoping I could trust him. "You see, the thing is, Father . . . I . . . we, me and Dylan, we've seen things. Seen them . . ."

"Seen them?" His expression was serious, but not judgmental.

I couldn't do this. He'd never believe me. Not in a million years. Who would? "Never mind." I shot to my feet, clutching Hunter's bag to my fluttering belly. "I—I think I made a mistake coming here."

Father Alvarez stood with me. Reaching across the void between us, he touched my arm. "No, you didn't. Please, Kaitlyn. You can talk to me in confidence. I won't tell anyone. Truly, you're safe here."

I swallowed hard and fought the urge to run. Where would I go? Back to my drunk mama and Keisha's ghost? To Dylan's house? Comforted by his touch, I let out something between a laugh and a sob and fell back into the chair. "I don't know how to say this, Father Alvarez. Maybe I'm going crazy. But Dylan and I, we've both seen Hunter and Keisha since the accident. We've seen their ghosts."

CHAPTER 6

FATHER ALVAREZ SAT THERE STARING AT ME. NOT A you're a-nut-case-crazy kinda stare, but a real, thoughtful, caring kinda stare. Then he opened a desk drawer and rummaged around in it before pulling out a small white box embossed with a little gold cross.

"What's that?" I asked, tilting my head toward the box.

"A gift." He held it out for me, but I didn't take it.

People I barely knew didn't give me gifts. So, why was he? I looked up at him, just now realizing tears were sliding down my cheeks. "Do you think I'm crazy?"

He shook his head, his lips in a firm, unwavering line. "No. I don't think you're crazy at all. I think you're suffering." He opened the box and pulled out a silver crucifix on a blue beaded chain. "And when you're suffering, the crucifix can give you spiritual strength and endurance."

There was nothing spiritual about me. "I don't even know if I believe in God, Father. So, I'm not sure how much good it'll do me." I couldn't believe I was saying this to a priest, but I'd never been one to sugarcoat things. Not to anyone. At least I was being honest.

"God, our Creator and Lord, can be known with

certainty, by the natural light of reason from created things. And He believes in you." Father Alvarez placed the crucifix in my hand, curled my fingers around the cool metal, and then studied my face. "Believe me, this will help . . . I don't know what you're seeing. It may be from grief or it may be something else . . ." He frowned.

"Something else? Like what?" I pushed back the growing panic in my chest that was threatening to bust its way out. What if he really believed in spirits and the supernatural? Could he actually help me?

"You tell me."

So, I told him about what we'd seen at church and about the Ouija board. Boy, did that make him scowl. "God commanded that mediums and all those who contact the dead and spirits should have no place among His people. Ouija boards aren't toys, Kaitlyn. They're very dangerous. You must be extremely careful."

"It was Dylan's idea. He figured if we could talk to them, ya know, find out why they're still here, then maybe we could . . ." I shrugged. What exactly had we hoped to do if we'd had an actual conversation? Tell them to move on? And go where? Keisha was so mad, she could start a fight in an empty house. And Hunter. He just seemed lost and scared—not the Hunter I knew. I guess neither was Keisha. They'd both been changed by death somehow. Keisha raving and furious, Hunter sad and lonely. How could I tell them to leave when I had no idea what was wrong and I didn't know where they were going?

"And you believe you saw them? Their spirits?" His brown eyes blazed with intensity, like he was trying to x-ray me with them.

"I know I did." I might sound bat-ass crazy, but I wasn't a liar.

He held his fingers together like a steeple and tapped

them together, lips pursed. "Ouija boards can let in . . . other things. Bad things."

"What kind of bad things? Spirits? Demons? Like in *The Exorcist*?" It was old, but Hunter had loved that film. I'd liked it too, but the book had freaked me out even more. Especially when the little girl had crawled down the stairs like some sort of human spider with her tongue licking in and out. So gross. I shivered.

The father gave me a hard stare, sort of like a teacher does when you know you've done something really stupid. "Please don't use it again. You should tell Dylan to get rid of it. If—if strange things continue to happen, the Catholic Church has set up a hotline for those in need of exorcisms."

"A hotline? For exorcisms?" My temperature rose at least ten degrees. Was he trying to make fun of me? "You're joking, right?"

"I'm quite serious. In the past few years, the Church has doubled the number of priests approved to do exorcisms and founded the hotline to help. But more often than not, the problems are not demonic."

Hair prickling on my scalp, I glared. "So you do think I'm just imagining things?"

He sat quietly for a moment, appearing to measure his words. "I believe you've been through a terrible tragedy, and in the process of coping, it is possible that your brain is making you think you're seeing things."

"What about Dylan? He's seen them, too. We can't both be imagining things!" Anger flared in my words, but I didn't care. If anyone would believe all this, it was supposed to be a Catholic priest.

"Remember, God is the Lord of the heavens and of the earth. He will care for you in all things." Father Alvarez squeezed my hand that held the crucifix. "It's only been a few days. Give it time. I hope this will bring you comfort. And I hope you'll need it for nothing more. *Dios te bendiga.* God bless you, *hija.*"

———

WHAT A WASTE OF TIME. I'd spent five hours breaking my butt on the cement in front of a church to be given a crucifix and sent on my way. Well, fine. If Father Alvarez wouldn't help me, then Dylan would. He didn't want to be haunted for the rest of his life any more than I did.

I sent Dylan a text and hoped he'd meet me at the corner of his street, which, thankfully, was a ten-minute walk from the church. It was only June but the sun blazed as hot as late July. For the first time, I was glad Hunter had made me put Dylan's number in my phone. "What if there's ever an emergency and you can't reach me, babe?" Little did he know.

My phone buzzed. It was Dylan.

I'll meet you there in ten minutes.

Of course he texted complete sentences. It was so Dylan.

Sweat trickled down between my shoulder blades as I rounded the corner to Dylan's street. He was already there, huddled in the shade of a massive oak, wearing his usual khaki shorts, polo shirt, and boat shoes. He didn't even like going on the river in his daddy's boat, but he still wore those stupid shoes. What a dork. Still, as my only living friend, I was glad he was there.

"Hey." He smiled as I walked up. A nervous, shaky smile. Dark circles hovered beneath his eyes. Maybe he'd had a long night, too.

"Hey." I didn't even bother trying to smile.

He nodded down the road toward his house. "Come on. I've got a plan, but I need to get my laptop."

"Why didn't you bring it with you?" I wasn't thrilled to be going anywhere near Dylan's ultra-beautiful house, let alone going inside. It'd only make me feel worse.

"Just come on and I'll get you a bottle of water."

Hot and too tired to argue, I trudged after Dylan. A cool drink and a few minutes in the A/C might be nice.

It took us nearly as long to cross the expanse that was Dylan's front yard as it had for me to walk to his street from the church. He led me around the side of the house and I shook my head at its size. I'd seen Dylan's house from the safety of Hunter's truck before, but never this close. A two-story brick mansion with a swimming pool on a five-acre lot. I eyed the clear blue water of the palm tree–surrounded pool and wondered what my daddy and mama had done so wrong to end up in a piece of crap trailer when a jerk like Dylan's daddy could end up in a gorgeous place like this. Our whole trailer would fit in that pool.

Dylan held the side door open for me. "Come on in," he said. That was the thing about Dylan. I'd give him that. He didn't act rich or arrogant, and he never cared that Hunter had grown up in a house half the size of his own. He was always friendly, even if he was sort of a nerd. I guess that's part of what Keisha loved about him. He was kind. And despite his daddy, he didn't seem to judge people.

He led me into a gourmet kitchen with granite counters like I'd seen on TV and pulled a couple bottles of water from the shiny chrome fridge. "Here." He handed me one and cracked open the other for himself. Then he gestured to his laptop, which was charging on the kitchen counter. "I've started doing more research, but I'm not sure which databases to use. It looks like there's a lot that hasn't been scanned into the digital archives yet. We need to go to the library."

"The library." The words had barely escaped my mouth when a fat, balding, ugly older version of Dylan wearing a Hawaiian shirt strolled into the kitchen. His jaw dropped open when he saw me.

I'd seen Mr. Anderson at school before, but had never had to talk to him. So, I smiled and tried to be polite. "Hello, Mr. Anderson."

Mr. Anderson looked me up and down, a scowl forming when he saw my faded Walmart T-shirt and the hunter-green canvas messenger bag slung around my shoulder. "What the hell is this?"

Dylan glared. "This is Kaitlyn. My friend."

"The girl from the accident," he nearly spat. "If you hadn't been dating that—"

"Don't even say it," Dylan snapped, his pale cheeks flushing pink.

Mr. Anderson shrugged. "I don't dump so much money in your college fund so you can date the town's lowlife."

I felt like I'd been slugged in the chest. I knew what folks thought about people who lived in trailer parks. I knew they whispered behind our backs and thought we were all losers or drug dealers or thieves. But I'd never had someone be so rude about it to my face. Not like this.

Dylan's face reddened, but he didn't say a word.

Mr. Anderson let out a humorless chuckle. "I let you get a taste of chocolate, sample something from the other side of the tracks. I paid for her funeral . . . It's done. Over." He gestured my way. "But don't push it."

Dylan's eyes were on fire, but his mouth was closed tight.

Why didn't Dylan stand up for Keisha or himself? Fury

boiled my blood. Well, if he wouldn't, I would. "You listen here—"

Mr. Anderson swung his piggy eyes to me. "No. You listen here, darlin'. I know your mama and I know your type. You need to stay away from my son and my money. That accident took care of one problem; you're not about to be another. Dylan'll be off to Boston for college in a year and will forget all about the likes of you." He shook his head and glared at Dylan. "I'll not have you trading in that black wild cat for this skinny piece of white trash."

I lost it. If blood could boil over, mine did. I shoved Dylan's daddy against the wall, my spit flying onto his face. "You're the piece of white trash. You disgusting pig." My words burned my tongue, but I didn't care. "Calling a dead girl that. Keisha. That's her name, Keisha. She was my friend and she loved your son."

"I don't give a rat's ass if she loved him or if he loved her. My son will not pollute our gene pool with the likes of her or you. Now get out of my house!" He loomed over me now, making me take a couple steps back.

Tears spilled down my cheeks and I was out of that house faster than a jackrabbit on crack. Calling me white trash was one thing—I wasn't stupid, I knew white trash when I saw it, too, and yeah, living in a trailer park pretty much defined it. Not that a kid could help where their mama made them live. But Keisha? Calling her names just because she was black. That was just wrong. Plain wrong. Her blackness didn't make her worth any less than him. It didn't make her worth less than any of us. She'd always said she had it harder than me because she was black. But I'd never believed her because she wasn't poor. Her daddy made a good living. She had two parents with two paychecks. I'd always argued that the color of her skin couldn't possibly make her life harder than mine. Maybe it had been. Maybe I'd been wrong.

I clenched my teeth and stormed down the street, Hunter's bag slapping me in the ass the entire way. White trash or not, I had a heart and a brain. Hunter knew it. He always told me I could be more than where I grew up. He'd always believed that—even when I didn't. My mama was my mama, he always said. She chose her life. And I could choose mine. I was me, not her. I was going somewhere. I was going to be someone. I *was* someone. Not trash. And I wasn't going to let some jerk with money talk like that about me or my friends.

I ran as fast as I could, snot and sweat and tears plastering hair to my face. A door slammed in the distance behind me and I heard Dylan calling my name, but I didn't stop. Screw him. And screw his daddy. I didn't need this crap. I'd deal with it on my own if I had to, but I wouldn't abandon Keisha or Hunter.

Rounding the corner to the next street, I leaned over panting, tears and sweat making little muddy puddles on the ground by my toes. I didn't want to go home, but where else could I go? I didn't have a shift at work until next week. Father Alvarez had done as much as he was willing, which was nothing except spout dogma at me. Dylan said something about the library, but it would take me forever to walk there. There was no place else to go but home. Home with the ghosts. Crap. I was screwed.

The soft rumble of an engine made me look up. A silver Chevrolet Malibu idled by the roadside. Dylan's car. Of course.

He rolled down his tinted window and a little belch of A/C hit me in the face. "Get in."

"No way in hell I'm getting in that car with you after

what your daddy just said. Do you think I'm crazy?" Ha. Maybe he did.

Dylan shoved open the passenger-side door and gestured for me to get in. "I'm sorry, Kaitlyn. I didn't expect him to be like that. Not after everything that's happened. Not with you." He shrugged. "At least not to your face."

"Why? Because I'm not black?" I spat.

He grabbed the steering wheel tight, his jaws clenched. I knew I was right.

"I guess being white trash is almost as bad," I growled, then I turned around and started walking away from him.

Dylan opened the door. "Kaitlyn. Stop." He stepped out of the car and walked over to face me. "I'm not like my father. Just like you're not your mother."

Ouch. That one hit near home, but I could still be pissed. Even if Dylan wasn't like his daddy.

He put his hands on my shoulders, keeping me in place. "And I'm sorry for what he said to you. For what he said about Keisha. You know it's not true. Not about you. Not about Keisha. None of it. He's just a racist jerk."

"A jerk?" I pulled away. He was more than a jerk. He was a redneck asshole who wore a suit during the week and got a big-ass paycheck, nothing more. "You didn't even stand up for Keisha." I was disgusted. Disgusted with Dylan. Disgusted with his father. Disgusted with this whole stupid town.

I started walking again. I didn't know where, but if it was away from Dylan's house and his nasty father then I was headed in the right direction.

Dylan came after me. Grabbing my arm, he spun me around. "Kaitlyn, stop," he pleaded. "I've tried to stand up to my dad before. All it ever gets me is a sore gut and an earful of his garbage. I'll be free of him soon enough. I just have to get through this next year."

His daddy hit him? Man, that was rough. At least that was something I'd never had to endure. My daddy had loved me . . . right up until the part when he left. But right now I was too pissed to really care about what Dylan had been through. "Yeah, you will. You get to leave this place. Go off to some fancy college and do something with your life. But what about me? I don't have a college fund. And with Hunter dead I don't even have a ride! All I got is a drunk-ass mama and a run-down trailer. I'm stuck here with the ghosts." It sucked . . . there had to be a way I could get out, even without Hunter. But I couldn't think about that. Not yet. First, I had to help him and Keisha, then I'd come up with a plan to escape this backward town.

"Do you think if I ever told my parents what we've seen they'd actually believe me?" He snorted. "My dad's only interested in what's best for business, and my mom's not much better. And as for college . . . I have to get into a good one because it makes them look better. They don't really care if I'm happy."

I clenched my teeth. Maybe he was just as alone in this whole mess as I was. Maybe we needed each other.

My heart softened, just a tad. "Why keep me around? Why not just forget about me and the accident? You're smart. Your daddy's rich. I'm sure you can figure out how to protect yourself from Keisha and Hunter until you leave town for good. You'll be just fine without me. You don't need my help."

Dylan looked at me. Not just a quick glance. He really looked at me. Sort of like how Hunter used to look at me. A look that told me I was important. A look that told me he cared. A look that let me know he really saw me—saw beyond the mess that was my life.

Before I could respond, his finger grazed my cheek. It lingered there awkwardly for a moment before he pulled a tear-encrusted strand of hair off my face and tucked it behind my ear.

Something unexpected twanged in my chest. It was a feeling meant for Hunter. Not Dylan. He wasn't even that cute. At least, he wasn't my type. Could we actually be becoming friends? Real friends? I sure couldn't let it be anything more than that.

A strange breeze gusted up, tussling my hair. I'd better be careful. Keisha could be watching. Hunter, too. I shoved the unwelcome longing aside and stepped away from him.

But Dylan acted like he didn't notice. "You're smart, Kaitlyn. I know you get straight As. You don't need somebody to help you get out of this town. You can do it all on your own."

I snorted. Getting straight As wasn't gonna do me much good in this town, and with all my money going to pay our bills, I sure as hell didn't see a way out just yet.

"You're right, Kaitlyn. I could do the research without you. But they're haunting us both. And I need a friend who understands what I lost in that accident." His eyes welled up, the memory of losing his girlfriend and best friend clear on his exhausted face. "Someone who knows what's really going on. And I can't bear the thought of Keisha and Hunt-*er* trapped here."

I stared at him and thought of Keisha. I thought of the anger and torment coming off her in my bedroom. I swallowed hard, wondering if Hunter'd been visiting Dylan at night while Keisha'd been tormenting me. Had Keisha been right when she was alive? Had Dylan secretly liked me, but kept it to himself because I was his best friend's girl-friend? But if that were true, why haunt me and not Dylan? And Keisha knew I'd never liked Dylan before. Not like that. I wouldn't have even considered it. He'd been Hunter's best friend since forever. And then he got together with Keisha. But now . . . I shooed away the notion. Stupid. And whether he liked me or not, we still needed answers. And he was the only one I knew who could help me get them.

"Kaitlyn, get in the car." He grabbed my hand and gave it a gentle squeeze. "Please."

The last place I wanted to be was in a car—especially in one with Dylan Anderson. But what choice did I have? It was either get in the car with him and take a fifteen-minute air-conditioned ride to the library, take a two-hour walk there in the heat, or go home to my drunk mama and haunted bedroom. Ugh. "Alright. Let's go."

A little smile cracked on Dylan's face, but I held up a finger. "Drive slowly, and don't take me near that tree."

"Deal."

CHAPTER 7

DYLAN HELD THE DOOR OPEN, THEN FOLLOWED ME INTO
the library. It was a place I knew well. Anytime I got off
work early or didn't want to be home with Mama, I came
here. At least when a coworker could drop me off and
Hunter could pick me up. I still didn't have a driver's
license on account of we couldn't afford a car, so getting a
license didn't make much sense. And since the accident, I
didn't think getting behind the wheel of a car sounded like
a very good idea anyway.

Dylan hopped on a computer and pulled up a Texas
historical database.

"What are we looking for?" I sat beside him in a nicked
wooden chair that made my butt hurt.

"I only went back ten years in my research before we
went out to photograph the tree. We need to look at local
records, further back." His fingers flew over the keys like
someone who was used to typing at lightning speed. I guess
Dylan wasn't a stranger to the library either or at least not
to doing research.

I peered over his shoulder at the words in the search
bar: *tree Harland car accidents death*

A shiver crawled over me like a giant roach at night. Lord only knows what we'd find with that combo.

A few articles popped up in the library's online archives. Dylan read and I skimmed the headlines over his shoulder.

"Two Local Teens Killed, Two Injured." It was the article about us, our four junior-year photos staring back at me. I remembered the day we took those pictures. It was the same day Hunter first said he wanted to marry me just as soon as we graduated. A swell of grief lodged itself in my throat, and I ripped my eyes away from the screen. I'd wanted to marry Hunter. I'd wanted to marry him more than anything in the world. That day had been one of the happiest in my life. How crazy that they used those pictures to memorialize the worst one.

I remember telling Mama that me and Hunter were going to get married one day. She was drunk, of course, and told me I was stupid. She'd said we were too young and didn't know a damn thing. I'd dropped it then, and decided to keep any plans I had for leaving between me and Hunter. I knew we were young. Maybe even too young. But if we'd gotten married, then we could've gotten out of this stupid town together. We'd have had each other. Now he was gone.

Sure, I knew I could still leave Harland on my own, but I'd never even consider doing it without Hunter. It'd take more work and a lot more saving, but if I wanted any chance at a life, I'd have to leave. Still, without Hunter, I didn't know if life was even worth living. I shut my eyes, willing myself not to cry. This was not the time or the place. My nostrils burned and I wiped my eyes with the back of my hand, trying to think of something else. Maybe I'd think of Mama. Thinking of her didn't make me cry; it made me mad.

I sure as hell didn't want to end up like her—a drunk in a broken-down trailer with smoke-stained clothes and no future. I let out a long sigh. I didn't know what I was going to do. I suppose I needed to focus on first things first—and that was figuring out why Keisha and Hunter were still here—so I didn't end up taking their spirits with me if I ever did get out of this godforsaken place.

Dylan's eyes were glued to the glowing screen. His fingers tapped the keys, and I watched the article dates moving further and further back in time. This was going to take a while.

After several minutes, he stopped on an article from 1928. "Look at this. It's when they named it the Devil's Tree. People around here thought it was haunted even back then."

I scanned the article, but it didn't really say much more than that. "Yeah. But haunted by what?"

"That's what we've got to find out." He nodded toward the screen and read aloud from another article:

A Caucasian woman, Agatha Archer, who lived near Harland, was found dead on September 23, 1926. Miss Archer, aged 22 at the time of her death, was found hanged on the large oak that stood near her home. There was suspicion of murder, but the police ruled Miss Archer's death as a suicide.

Holy crap. "That poor woman. Why would they have suspected anything other than suicide? Were white people ever lynched?"

"I don't know. Seems like it would've been a suicide." Dylan typed a few words into the search bar. Several links popped up, and Dylan skimmed them.

"Hey, look at this. It's an article in the *Montgomery Advertiser* from 2017 about lynching." He pointed at the screen.

Lynching is the unjustified setting aside of judicial due process for mob vengeance. Mob violence in the form of lynching brings law into contempt. President Reagan once stated: "without law, there can be no freedom, only chaos and disorder. And without freedom, law is but a cynical veneer for injustice and oppression." Lynching is, by definition and by its nature, lawless.

Hovering over Dylan's shoulder, I skimmed the rest of the article:

While some whites were lynched for murder or stealing cattle, there is another important reason many were lynched. Many whites were lynched for helping blacks or being anti-lynching . . . Ninety percent of whites were lynched in nine states mostly in a swath from Montana to Nebraska, Oklahoma, Arkansas and Texas.

I finished reading and shook my head. "Wow. I had no idea."

"Me either," said Dylan, which was surprising on account of Dylan usually seemed to know most things. "But if it wasn't a suicide and she really was lynched, then maybe that's why she's still here. The tree really could be haunted."

I pushed off a shiver and leaned back in my chair.

"We need to find out more about the tree to see if any other events have happened there. Maybe other accidents related to the area." Dylan typed in a couple more keywords and scanned the links. "Look." Dylan pointed to a new article that had popped up on the screen. "Here's another one. A black truck reportedly ran someone off the road right by the Devil's Tree. The other driver was killed in the crash, the passenger survived. But they never found evidence of the truck."

The hairs on my arms and the back of my neck stood up. "A black truck? What year?"

"It was 1927. The year after she died." Dylan's voice sounded hollow and soft and made me tremble.

I tried to shake off the creepiness factor with some

common sense. "Did they even have pickup trucks back then?"

Dylan finished reading the article and clicked the print button. "Yep. The Ford Model T Runabout came out in 1925. It was replaced by a Model A in 1928."

"And you know this how?" The amount of random knowledge rattling around in Dylan's brain amazed me sometimes.

He shrugged. "Hunt-*er*" he gave me a quick glance, then went back to scrolling through articles while he talked "loved trucks. I learned a lot going to car shows with him."

Hunter had loved his cars and trucks, that's for sure. But I didn't know they actually learned anything going to all those car shows. "So a truck ran someone off the road back in 1927. Other folks have seen phantom pickups out that way. I wonder if 1927 was the first time?" I gulped down spiders of fear that tickled my throat. "Was it the same truck that chased us?" My voice came out as a whisper. "And if it was, then what does a truck chasing people have to do with Agatha and the tree?"

"I have no idea, but—"

A nearby wail broke my concentration, making me and Dylan jump, colliding into each other. His skin was soft and warm and comforting. I pulled away from him, and doing my best to ignore him, I looked for the source of the wailing.

A little girl, no more than five, looking totally lost, stood between two nearby bookshelves. Tears streamed down her face, pasting her glossy black hair to her little rosy cheeks.

Boy, did I know how she felt. Alone. Scared. Lost.

Pulling myself out of my own funk, I set my bag beside Dylan, walked over and knelt down in front of her. "Hey there, sweetie, what's the matter?"

Sniffing, she tried to control her tears. "I—I want my mama. I can't find her."

"I know how that feels." I smiled and reached out my hand to her. "Let me help you."

She hesitated, but only for a second. Her little hand was sticky in mine—from sweat or a morning sweet I wasn't sure—but that didn't matter. I curled my fingers around hers and walked her over to the librarian's desk, glad there was someone I could actually help.

"What's the matter, darlin'? Lost your mommy?" the librarian asked.

She sucked yellowish snot into her nose and nodded her head, ponytail flopping. "Uh-huh."

Just as the librarian was about to make a circuit around the library, a frantic-looking woman came rushing out of the romance section. "Lola? Lola!" Her eyes tracked to the little girl and she headed straight for us.

"Mama." Lola pried her hand from mine and launched herself at the woman.

"Oh, thank God, Lola." The woman pulled the girl to her in a massive hug. I smiled, remembering when my mama used to hug me like that.

The teary-eyed woman looked at me. "Thank you."

I gave her a little smile, happy I could do something useful, then turned back to find Dylan leaning against the table, watching me. A strange mix of emotions flashed over his face: sadness, tenderness, love?

I frowned and walked back over to him. "What?"

He shook his head, a little grin still stuck on his face. "There's more to you than people see, Kaitlyn. Even Hunter didn't see it all."

Really? I didn't know Dylan had been looking. Maybe Keisha was right to be jealous. I swallowed back the ball of why-did-Hunter-have-to-die pain forming in my throat. I didn't want another guy knowing me. Not that well. Not like that.

"You read too much into things." I sounded way more bitter than I felt, but I didn't want Dylan thinking he could get too close. "I'm just a trailer park girl." The old feelings of my hopeless loser life flooded over me. Never mind my great grades and the possible scholarships my teachers said I'd get. None of that seemed to matter now.

Dylan frowned. "Just because your father ran off and you live in a trailer doesn't mean that's where you'll be forever."

"That's easy for you to say. Your daddy owns more than half the town."

He looked me straight in the eye. "Not everything is easy for me, Kaitlyn."

"Like Keisha?" I growled. I felt bad for being mean, but Dylan had everything so easy. "I'm sure it took a lot of guts to date a black girl just to piss off your daddy."

He grunted out a sigh, and a sort of defeated, disgusted look took over his face. "I didn't date Keisha to piss off my dad. I wouldn't do that to Keisha or anyone. I really cared about her."

"Then why did you date her? She was my best friend until you came along." Wow. That sounded bitter. Well, maybe it was. When Keisha started dating Dylan, my best friend had all but disappeared. She was too busy with "her man."

"II didn't mean to hurt your friendship . . . I dated her because she was nice and smart. I liked that she didn't care that my parents had money. I liked that she didn't care that your mom didn't. Or that Hunter's parents drank too much. She liked us for who we were. Not for what we had or didn't have."

That was a knife in the chest. He was right. That's

what I'd liked—no, loved—about Keisha, too. She'd really been able to see the good in people and nothing else mattered—not color, not money, not grades.

He took his glasses off, rubbed the bridge of his nose, then looked at me. "So, no. I didn't date her to piss off you or my dad or anyone else. I dated her because she really liked me for who I am. Maybe I listened to my father's racist slurs or took a few slaps one too many times on account of Keisha's color, but I knew we'd get away . . ." He shrugged. "Or I thought we would. Before the accident . . . Anyway, I don't care what he says about you, either. And I'm not going to ditch you because of his elitist BS."

I never knew people could be so hateful just because someone was black. Keisha was my best, oldest friend. And her parents were good people. I was beginning to think Keisha's life hadn't been quite as easy as I thought it'd been. Or Dylan's either.

I crossed my arms over my chest and studied his face. I'd never seen Dylan without his glasses. His eyes were clear and kind and honest. Sweet even. It was like I was seeing him for the first time. Really seeing him. Like Tobey Maguire in *Spider Man*—he looked sort of dorky with his glasses, but after he got bit by the spider and took them off . . . well, he was hot. I swallowed, my eyes traveling over Dylan's face. He had stubble. I didn't even know Dylan shaved, not that I'd ever thought about it. But sure enough, there was a little bit of stubble growing in, making his jaw look strong and angular. His lips full and soft.

I yanked myself away from thinking of Dylan's lips. That was so not gonna happen. "So, you think it's Agatha Archer keeping people at that tree?"

"I don't know, but we're going to find out."

"And how are we gonna do that?"

Dylan grabbed a couple articles off the library printer. "We're going back to the tree, but this time we're going to take the Ouija board with us."

―――――

HANDS firmly on the wheel and eyes on the road, Dylan kept to the speed limit on the old gravel road that led us to the Devil's Tree.

Nausea wormed its way up my throat with every bump of the road. And it wasn't car sickness. It was something in my gut warning me. Warning me I was headed for trouble. I was terrified and freaked out and heartsick. I couldn't believe I was going along with this. We were actually going to use the Ouija board again—never mind Father Alvarez's warnings or what happened last time—and try to contact the spirit of a dead woman? At the Devil's Tree? Oh. My. God. "You're three gallons of crazy in a two-gallon bucket, Dylan Anderson, you know that, right?"

Dylan gave me a sideways glance and smiled. He actually smiled.

I reached right over and slapped his leg—hard.

"Ow." He scowled and his fingers gripped the steering wheel tighter.

Good. He should be scowling.

"What else do you suggest we do, Kaitlyn? I couldn't find any more articles on the tree or why they're trapped there. Until our accident, nothing had been written about it since Old Joe died four years ago. That's why I went out there in the first place: to find new information and write an article for the paper."

"Yeah. A lot of help that did any of us," I snapped, fiddling with the little tag at the edge of my messenger bag.

Boy, was I being mean. But the last thing I wanted was to end up dead.

A look of guilt washed over Dylan's face and he bit his lower lip. "I didn't mean for this to happen, Kaitlyn. None of it. But I can't change the past. All I can do is try to shape the future. And if we want to set Hunter and Keisha free and stop them from haunting us, then we have to find out if the woman who died there is behind it. And if she is, why exactly she's chasing and killing people."

We drove in silence after that. What more was there to say about a wronged soul striking out at the living? We pulled up to the tree around noon. My stomach lurched at the sight of it and gave a soft rumble. I couldn't remember the last time I ate, but there was no way I was having anything to eat until after this Dylan-sanctioned ritual was behind us.

The place didn't look nearly as scary in the daytime. The tree was still twisted and gnarled and dark, but there were no freaky winds or black pickup trucks.

We climbed out of the car and I followed Dylan toward the old oak. A rusty chain still hung from one of its branches, and the trunk was still wrapped in chain link. There were no new hack marks far as I could tell. After what'd happened to us and Old Joe, I doubted anyone would try to touch it let alone cut it down again anytime soon.

I looked up at the tree's thick branches and wondered which one Agatha Archer had been hanged from. I shivered. Having the life choked out of you didn't seem like a pleasant way to die.

"Okay. Let's set it up here." Dylan pulled the Ouija board from his backpack and opened it on a patch of dried grass a couple feet from the base of the tree.

Stuffing my hand in an outer pocket of my bag, I

squeezed the crucifix Father Alvarez had given me. It poked into my hand, but I squeezed harder, praying to God I wasn't gonna need it.

Dylan sat cross-legged in front of the Ouija board, placed his fingers lightly on the planchette, and looked up at me expectantly. "Come on, Kaitlyn. This is why we came here. I can't do it by myself."

I huffed, pulled the bag off from around my shoulder, and sat down opposite him. "Fine, but if this doesn't bring us a single step closer to sending Keisha and Hunter on their way, then I'm done with using this thing." I gestured to the board with my chin, but placed my fingers lightly on the pointer.

Dylan focused on the Ouija board and took a deep breath. Shoot, for a smart boy he was really getting into this. "I'm calling out to the spirit of Agatha Archer. Miss Archer, if you're still here, Kaitlyn and I want to talk with you."

I noted his politeness. I supposed that was a good thing. He'd said it would be different this time. That we'd be respectful, quiet. That it would help keep us safe. I remembered what Father Alvarez said about Ouija boards and unleashing spirits. Unfriendly spirits. Yeah, Ms. Archer wasn't likely to be my new bestie.

As if in response to my thoughts about Agatha, the sky grew suddenly dark and a breeze picked up, rustling the branches overhead.

We waited.

But there were no sounds. No voices. There weren't even any normal outdoor sounds. No birds, no squirrels, no frogs. Nothing but the whispering breeze and rustling branches.

The breeze mingled with the hungry silence like it was waiting to gobble us up.

Fingers still on the pointer, I felt the air grow cool like winter was coming. My breath caught in my throat and my belly took a dip. It was either fear or something was coming.

"Agatha Archer," Dylan's voice cracked, then steadied into a slight quiver. "We know you died here. We know you were killed at this tree. If your spirit remains, please talk to us. We want to know what really happened to you."

The pointer started twitching then.

We both stared at the Ouija board. "Is that you, Ms. Archer?"

The planchette moved slowly at first, circling from *yes* to *no*, then over the alphabet. It slid over to me, then back to the letters. It moved from H to U to N to T to E to R.

"Hunter," I gasped, fresh tears springing into my eyes. "Hunter, are you okay? I miss you. I"

The pointer began moving again. Faster.

G – O.

N – O – W.

S – H – E – S.

C – O – M – I – N – G.

G – O.

N – O – W.

G – O.

N – O – W.

G – O.

N – O – W.

The message repeated itself over and over again.

Tears streaming, I tried to pry my hands from the pointer, but it was like an invisible force kept my fingers in place. "Who's doing this?"

"Keisha," Dylan called out. "If you can hear me, don't hurt Kaitlyn. We want to help you. You and Hunter both."

Suddenly the planchette stopped and an icy cold dread filled the air, settling into the pit of my stomach.

The pointer began moving again, and the temperature dropped until our breaths came out in ghostly puffs.

T – O – O.

L – A – T – E.

"Who is this?" Dylan demanded, sounding more angry than afraid. "Why did you chase us? Why are Keisha and Hunter trapped here?"

A rumble of thunder crashed overhead, and the sky darkened further. A blinding pain, like a jolt of electricity, shot up my arms, and I tried to yank my hands free of the planchette. But they were held in place. I couldn't scream. Couldn't move. Couldn't run.

Dylan jerked backward, his teeth jarring against each other so hard I could hear his jaw crack. His eyes rolled back in his head, looking like boiled eggs streaked with bluish veins, and a low, hissing voice escaped from his throat. Something wicked was here. Something evil.

"Who dares disturb my grave?" The voice coming from Dylan was fierce and mean and female.

I felt the blood drain out of my face and race through my veins. This wasn't happening. It couldn't be.

The egg-like white eyes rolled toward me, darting around my face. And for a moment—just for a moment—I swear I saw the face of an angry woman looking back at me. "What do you want, girl?" she hissed through Dylan's lips.

Holy crap. Dylan was possessed by a dead woman.

"Agatha Archer?" I squeaked, barely able to breathe I was so scared.

"Yes," she seethed, the word slippery and sharp at the same time.

"We just want to help our friends." My voice was low and weak and full of fear.

"You and your friends should not have come here. You should not have soiled my grave. They now belong to Alastor."

"Alastor?"

A hoarse cackle burst from Dylan's mouth. "Alastor will have his sacrifice."

"Sacrifice?" What on earth was she talking about? I tried to grab for the crucifix in my messenger bag, but my fingers were still plastered to the planchette.

The voice cackled again, making Dylan's mouth contort into a leer. "Every witch has her secrets."

As soon as the last syllable escaped his lips, Dylan's eyes rolled back in his head and he collapsed to the ground.

CHAPTER 8

DYLAN PLOPPED ON THE EDGE OF MY BED, OPENED HIS laptop, and typed in his password, the screen casting an eerie blue glow on his face.

"How can you seriously just sit there and do research when that—that dead witch-woman just possessed you?" My voice cracked with thinly veiled hysteria.

Dylan glanced up at me, then back at the keyboard. "I'm fine, Kaitlyn. It didn't hurt."

"Are you crazy? She was inside you. You were possessed! Your eyes . . ." I shuddered. "And do you know what she said?"

"I told you I do." He took a pause from typing. "It was weird." He weighed his words before he spoke, like he was trying to be sure they were the right ones. "It was kind of like someone pulled some gauze over my mind. I could see and hear and feel, but I wasn't fully there. She was at the controls. And I could feel her anger." He looked away for a moment, almost in a daze, then shook his head and looked up at me.

"Yeah, but what was she angry about?"

"Kaitlyn . . ." Mama's voice floated through my door

and I cringed. I wasn't so worried about what she'd think of Dylan being in my bedroom. I was more worried about what Dylan would think of Mama.

She pushed open my squeaky bedroom door without knocking. Her hair looked like it hadn't been washed in a week, and her wrinkled T-shirt and grungy jeans in at least that long. And she'd lost weight, too. I needed to get back to work and make sure she was eating.

As soon as she saw Dylan, she stopped and took a long drag from her cigarette. Last I'd heard she'd quit smoking. Looked like that had lasted about as long as the time she tried to quit drinking.

"Hi, Mama. You remember Dylan Anderson, don't you?" I tried to act like I wasn't pissed she'd just barged into my personal space or worried that she looked so frail.

As she took another drag off her cigarette, her eyes narrowed. "Sure I do. You're Hunter's friend." She staggered just inside the doorway, scowling from me to him and back again. "What're you doin' in my daughter's bedroom?"

Great. It wasn't even half past eight on a weeknight and Mama was already drunk. Typical. "We're working on a project, Mama." I gestured to Dylan's laptop.

"We're doing some research, Ms. Karly." Dylan smiled at her, trying to be friendly.

"Humpf." She took another drag. "Looks mighty cozy for research."

"Really, Mama? It's not like we have any place else to work." I scowled right back at her. She'd never complained about Hunter staying over. And who was she to talk? She'd had several different men parade through our trailer since my daddy left. I just locked my door, but never complained about it. So long as they didn't hurt me or her, I couldn't have cared less. "Besides, it's none of your business who's in my bedroom any more than it is my business who's in yours."

She took two quick steps forward and grabbed my jaw, hard. Not something I'd ever have expected Mama to do. "You watch your mouth, Kaitlyn Karly. That Hunter was a good boy. You've barely even cried over him since he got killed . . . and now you've gone right off and replaced him. With his friend, too. I raised you better than that. Don't you dare go off and be like your daddy."

I felt like I'd been slapped in the face and yanked my jaw away from her. I jumped off the bed, forcing Mama back toward my open bedroom door. "You have no idea what you're talking about, Mama. No idea. Whatsoever. You're too drunk to know what's going on in your own life let alone mine," I spat. I knew it'd hurt her feelings, but I didn't care. "You couldn't even be bothered to go to their funerals so why do you give a crap about who I have in my bedroom?"

"That's right. That's me. Nothing but your drunk mama." She glared at me. "Go on, then, be a whore. See how far it'll get you." And with that, she spun on her heels, walked out of my room, and slammed the bedroom door right in my face.

Tears of embarrassment and shame burned my eyes. I kept my back to Dylan. I didn't want to face him, but I couldn't bolt from my room either. I couldn't leave Dylan alone in my trailer with her. And I didn't want to deal with Mama. Not like this. Besides, she'd be gone to the bar soon enough.

"Kaitlyn." Dylan was behind me now. He squeezed my shoulder, but I pulled away.

"Don't." I sniffed back tears that I couldn't stop from spilling down my face and onto my shirt.

From the front room, Mama bellowed, "Don't worry

about me, you little whore, I'll be out . . . all night! Like mother, like daughter." Then the trailer door slammed shut.

I sucked back a sob. I had to get out of here. I couldn't keep living like this. Hunter'd seen her this way more than once. And he'd promised we'd get out. He'd promised. Now he was dead and I was trapped. I couldn't even imagine how I'd manage leaving on my own. Especially not with all this crazy ghost crap going on. But there had to be a way. There had to . . .

"Kaitlyn." Dylan spun me around to face him.

I shoved him away, but he just pulled me into his embrace. His arms wrapped around me and I inhaled the soft, mingled scent of Abercrombie and sweat. A warm, comforting scent. I let loose then, falling into his arms. All the tears and hurt and anger that'd been building up about Hunter and Keisha dying, about Daddy leaving, about Mama being such a mean-ass drunk. They all came pouring out of me. Life just sucked. It was all so unfair. And I hated it.

I'm not sure how long I cried. It felt like hours. But Dylan didn't complain. Not once. He just sat me on my bed and held me and stroked my hair, telling me it would all turn out alright somehow. When my tears had finally dried, and my nose was so stuffed up I couldn't breathe, it felt like a great big cavern of emptiness had opened up inside my chest—but emptiness was better than pain.

"What are we gonna do?" My voice cracked.

Dylan tucked a few stray strands of tear-sticky hair behind my ear and smiled. "First, I'm going to go and get us both some water. Then we're going to find out exactly who or what is at that tree. We might not be able to change our parents. But we can do something to help Hunter and Keisha. And once we've helped them, then we can focus on getting ourselves out of this town and away from our parents."

"Do you really think that's possible? For me, I mean?" I looked up at him, a twinge of hope fluttering in my heart.

"Of course it is, Kaitlyn. You don't need a college fund to get away from this place. You work hard. You get good grades. I don't have any doubt you can leave as soon as you graduate. We both just have to get through all this." He gestured at the Devil's Tree research on his computer, then put his arm around me. "Then we have to get through the next school year and we're done. You can get out of here."

I took a deep breath and smiled up at him. "I sure hope you're right."

Two glasses of water later, I took a seat beside Dylan on my bed and wrapped myself in Gran's old quilt wondering what Dylan would dig up next.

He angled the laptop toward me. I read what he'd brought up on the screen, then looked at him. "The *Demonicpedia*? Really? It sounds like something straight out of that TV show *Supernatural*. Is it even legit?" It was bizarre enough that we were dealing with ghosts, and maybe a witch-ghost, but why on God's good earth was he researching demons?

"It's legit enough. Now, look." Dylan scrolled down a couple lines to a name: Alastor.

I froze. Alastor. That was the name the witch had told us. "Alastor's a demon?"

"Looks that way. And listen to this." He looked back at the screen and read aloud. "Alastor. From Christian demonology. A possessing entity brought on by a curse. A cruel demon called the executioner."

As if in response to his words, thunder rolled overhead and rain began to spatter against our thin-walled trailer. We both glanced out the window, then looked at each other. I pulled my ratty quilt tight around my shoulders and yanked my messenger bag up onto the bed with me and Dylan kept reading. "An executioner. He is associated with sin that passes down through generations . . . He is very cruel."

Great. Just what we needed—a cruel demon.

"What if somehow that demon is bound to that tree? What if he's the one causing the truck to chase people off the road? What if he's the one killing them?" Dylan stared hard at the screen as if it would answer.

It was too terrible to think about. Ghosts were one thing, but witches and demons? What would Father Alvarez say about this? "I don't know, Dylan. It's—it's . . ." It's crazy. Pure and simple crazy. I'd never really had time to think about God or the devil. My life had been about work and school and Hunter. It'd been about surviving. It wasn't about ghosts and witches and demons.

"It's a stretch, I know. But that woman, that—that witch. She knew something. She had this sort of sick, twisted pleasure from the fact Hunter and Keisha are trapped. She was angry, too. But I also felt this lack of control—not mine, hers."

"She did say something about him keeping his sacrifices." I swallowed. "But what does she have to do with Alastor?"

"I don't know." Dylan closed the lid to his laptop and pulled out the Ouija board.

"Oh, no. No way. There's no way in hell I'm getting on that thing again. You're insane, Dylan Anderson. Totally nuts!" I kicked the Ouija board away from Dylan and sent it flying under my desk. "Just don't forget to take it with you when you leave this time."

He grabbed my hands hard and looked at me. "We need more information, Kaitlyn. There's no one to ask at the library. No parent or teacher who'll know the answers. And we need answers. We need to know what connection Agatha has to Alastor. It's the only way we can really figure out what's going on."

"And who are you planning to contact now? A demon?"

Dylan scowled and gave a slight shake of his head. "We need to talk to Keisha and Hunter. I think they're bound here because of Agatha or Alastor. I'm not sure which, but maybe they can give us answers if we ask the right questions."

"Right. You can ask away, but there's no way I'm getting back on that thing." I huffed, wearily eyeing the board lying a few feet away, fear trampling my heart.

"Fine. Then maybe this will work." Dylan leaned forward. His breath hitched—just for a second—then he pulled me to him and pressed his lips against mine.

He tasted like salt and mint and electricity. A zap shot from my lips straight down to my . . . Oh, hell no. No way. I stiffened and pulled back. "What are you doing?"

"They'll respond to this."

"I want Keisha's attention, but I don't want her to kill me." I didn't want to hurt her either, or Hunter. My heart battled against my mind, fighting this strange new urge I had to kiss Dylan.

"Kiss me, Kaitlyn. If you want them to come without using the Ouija board, then this is the only way to be sure we'll get their attention."

Maybe he was right. I wasn't about to use the Ouija board again, and kissing me was bound to make Keisha jealous. I wasn't sure I should do this—kiss Dylan—but he'd been so sweet and kind tonight—despite Mama. Despite me having nothing. Maybe Keisha'd been right to love him the way she did. No. I couldn't think like that. If I kissed him, it would be to get Keisha's attention. That's all. And it seemed like it was a sure-fire way to make them come.

I grabbed on to Hunter's bag, feeling the crucifix through the canvas pocket, then leaned forward, closed my eyes, and let myself kiss Dylan.

For a second I felt his scruffy face against my cheek, then I was lost in the warmth of his lips. His hands traveled over my shoulders, through my hair. His mouth moved over mine, soft and warm and sweet. I let myself go then. I wanted this. I wanted it more than I realized. I kissed him back.

I'd never wanted to kiss Dylan before. I may have looked at his soft lips and strong jaw, but shoot, I'd never even imagined what it would be like to actually kiss him. And I certainly didn't expect it to be like this. No wonder Keisha'd been so into him. Dylan Anderson was a fantastic kisser.

A wail interrupted our kiss and something threw me against the bedroom wall, away from Dylan. Away from the warmth and safety of his arms.

Keisha. Burned and bloody and madder than a hornet with its nest on fire. "You bitch." Keisha clutched my neck, and her once perfect nails dug into my skin. Her icy fingers pressed into my throat, choking the air out of me.

I gasped, and let out a strangled cry, my feet rising off the floor in Keisha's too-strong grip. I tried to speak, but couldn't get a word out.

"Stop it, Keisha." Hearing Dylan's voice was all it took to distract her.

She loosened her grip, and I shoved my hand into my bag, grabbed the crucifix, and swung it into the side of her ice-cold head. She screamed and shot away from me to the opposite side of my tiny room, angry eyes fixed on Dylan.

"How could you kiss *her?*" she seethed. "You said you barely even liked her. You said you only tolerated her for the sake of that weeping, overly protective thing." She jerked her thumb over her shoulder to Hunter. "But you lied to me, Dylan. Every time I asked if you really liked Kaitlyn, you said no. Liar! All you were doing was covering up your real feelings."

Hunter was a shadow of his living self. Hunched and crying, he lurked in the corner of my tiny room. "I'm sorry, Kaitlyn. So, so sorry. Sorry about everything." His voice was weak, tattered.

A wave of guilt crashed over me. How could I have kissed Dylan? It must've ripped Hunter's heart apart. And Keisha. I hadn't wanted to hurt her either.

"Oh, please." Keisha rolled her eyes and glared at Dylan. "Get out of my way, Dylan, or I'll hurt you."

Dylan stood up then and faced her, tears brimming. "I don't believe that. You won't hurt me, Keisha. I loved you. And you loved me."

Hands on her hips, Keisha's eyes softened. "Maybe I did. You showed me white guys aren't all bastards. You showed me I could be myself no matter what. You showed me people could overcome hatred. But what does that matter now? I'm dead and you—you're alive and kissing *her.*"

"I did it because I knew it'd make you come. That's all." Dylan's eyes were sad, pleading.

Ouch. And I'd given myself over to that kiss. What an ass. I was sorry I'd even done it—especially considering poor Hunter. Guilt shot through my heart all over again, and I hoped he hadn't seen the kiss.

Keisha crossed her arms over her chest, just like she always did when she was pissed. "And I'm supposed to believe that?"

"Keisha, come on. We needed to talk to you and Kaitlyn wouldn't use the board again. You know me. You know how I felt about you."

"Felt," she spat. "Exactly."

"Stop. Just for a second. Stop and listen to yourself. Stop and think. You know what I went through with my father to be with you. You know I wouldn't have done that if I didn't really care." He took a step closer to her, but stopped just shy of touching her. "And I still care, Keisha. Do you really want to be stuck here on earth forever?" He looked at Hunter. "Or you, Hunt? We were best friends. I don't want you trapped here. I want to help you. I want you to move on and find peace. We both do."

"So you can be with her," Keisha said, glaring at me over Dylan's shoulder. "Agatha's right. You men are all the same. They use you, then piss all over you as they're walking away." She scowled, her teeth gleaming in her bloody, broken face.

"That's not true, and you know it. Don't listen to what Agatha says. She's probably the one keeping you here! All Kaitlyn and I want is for you and Hunter to be at peace."

Hunter moved closer to us then. Tears streaked his pale cheeks, but he no longer cried. "How can you help us? We're trapped."

I crawled over the rumpled covers toward the edge of my bed. "Hunter." Pain punched me hard in the chest. Even burned and dead, he was my Hunter. I couldn't leave him to keep on suffering. "We know about that woman. We know about Agatha. We think she was a witch. She died at that tree; she was lynched. And somehow a demon is involved. His name is Alastor."

Keisha wailed.

Hunter cowered, hands over his ears. "Don't say his

name. Don't say it or he'll come. He'll hurt you. He'll hurt us all."

I crept around Dylan, who reached out a hand to stop me.

"It's okay," I said. "I need to talk to him."

Slowly, he let his hand drop from my arm. "Be careful."

Crouching beside Hunter's battered, translucent spirit, I willed him to look at me. "Hunter." My voice was soft, gentle. The way it used to be when it was just him and me alone. Alone and sharing our deepest secrets. "Hunter, talk to me. Like we used to." Tears choked my words, but I couldn't help it. Hunter'd been the love of my life. He knew more about me than anyone. Ever. "Please."

He looked at me then, his face bruised and bloodied and burned. "Kaitlyn." He reached out his hand to touch my face. I closed my eyes, but only felt a chill where his fingers should have been.

"I'm here," I whispered and opened my eyes. "I don't want to let you go, but I will if it means you'll have peace. I want to help you. I want you to be free. I want you to be happy."

"He'll never let us go. I thought you could help, but . . ." Hunter, always strong and confident and sure of himself in life, was the opposite in death. Weak, afraid, pitiful. Trapped. "She made a deal, Kaitlyn. Agatha made a deal to avenge herself."

"Against who?" Tears cascaded down my cheeks. How I missed his touch, his warmth, his love. I had the stupid bag he'd given me, but I didn't have him. Had he seen me kiss Dylan? If he had, it must have hurt him so damn much. And I'd enjoyed it. A new swirl of confusion and guilt wrapped itself around my heart and squeezed.

Hunter gazed at me, his eyes clearer than I'd seen them

since he'd passed. "I heard her talking to Keisha. And whispering to herself. She murmured through the night. All night. Every night. She keeps saying his name over and over again."

I reached out, wanting to take him in my arms, but my fingers tingled with cold where his body should have been. "Whose name, Hunter?" I asked, my hand as cold as the spot where Hunter stood. "Whose name?"

He looked at me with sad eyes that pierced my heart. "If there's any hope at all, find Henry Willis. Maybe he can help you."

A boom of thunder clapped overhead and a flash of bluish-purple lightning illuminated my room. When the lightning was gone, so were Keisha and Hunter.

CHAPTER 9

I OPENED MY EYES AND STARED AT THE YELLOWING floral wallpaper peeling from my bedroom walls. It'd been the best night of sleep I'd had since the accident. If there had been an accident. Maybe it'd all been a terrible dream. A nightmare. Wouldn't that be nice? I'd get up, get dressed, and get ready for Hunter to take me to work. Then, after work, Hunter would pick me up and we'd grab dinner and do homework together or dream about our future. As tedious as the Food Mart was sometimes, I missed that life. I missed the rhythm and certainty of it.

I rolled over and saw Dylan sound asleep on the tattered Care Bear sleeping bag I'd had since second grade, his legs stretched way past the bag's ratty end. I nearly laughed, but didn't. It would've been better if it had been a dream. Then Hunter would be in bed curled up beside me and Dylan wouldn't be here sprawled out on my bedroom floor in his place.

Dylan hadn't gone home. He'd told his parents he was staying with some friend visiting from college. I'm not sure if they believed him, but he didn't seem too worried. I'd taken the bed. He'd taken the floor. Mama didn't come home last night, so we didn't have to worry about her calling me names and accusing Dylan of betraying his best friend. And whether I wanted to admit it or not, I was glad he'd stayed.

With a sigh, I flopped on my back and wondered how I could've slept at all when we knew some witch or demon was responsible for keeping Hunter and Keisha and probably many other poor souls trapped at that tree. Maybe it was because Dylan had been here. Or maybe it was the crucifix I had wrapped around my wrist.

Dylan stretched with a cute little groan. No, darn it. I was not gonna think of his groans or anything else about him as cute. Especially not after seeing Hunter so sad last night. Or after Dylan telling Keisha he'd only kissed me to lure her here. What a jerk. Still, neither of us should have enjoyed it.

Propping himself up on his elbows, Dylan peered over the edge of my bed, his hair poking up at odd angles. "Morning." He smiled, that ultra-cute strong-jawed smile I'd seen the other day.

There was that word again. Cute. Nothing was supposed to be cute to me except for Hunter and kittens and little kids with chocolate smeared all over their faces. It was too soon to be into another guy. Especially when that guy was my dead boyfriend's best friend. "Morning," I scowled and pulled my sheet to my chin.

"What's the matter?" He plopped himself on the edge of my bed and my pulse sped up like a jackrabbit on steroids.

"Aside from ghosts and maybe a witch-ghost or demon keeping our exes here and you kissing me as bait?" I snapped. "Not much."

"Come on, Kaitlyn. Do you think if I'd told Keisha I

wanted to kiss you she'd have even listened to us for half a second?"

Wait. He'd wanted to kiss me? A little throb of desire tickled me down low, but I did my best to ignore it. Maybe he was lying to me, just like he'd lied to Keisha. But even if he was telling the truth, I shouldn't want him to kiss me. I should still be thinking about Hunter and Keisha. Not Dylan.

He ran his hands through his dirty blond hair and slid on his glasses. "Besides, we have more important things to worry about today than kissing. If we want to end their entrapment and put an end to all of the people getting run off the road by whatever is in that tree, then we need more information. We need to find out about Henry Willis."

Dylan was right. The last thing I needed to fret over was a stupid kiss. We had to figure out who Henry Willis was and how he could help us free our friends.

We made a quick Starbucks run—the first I'd made without Hunter, which was hard. Real hard. Even without him here, Hunter was everywhere. He lingered in my mind and my memories. Even my white chocolate mocha wasn't the same without him. Still, when I was stressed, I couldn't say no to a white chocolate mocha. Besides, it was Dylan's treat. And after all the crap he'd put me through with that Ouija board, I wasn't gonna turn down a Starbucks. I didn't think Hunter would mind anyway. It was only coffee.

A few minutes later, coffee in hand, we were back at the library and Dylan was in an intense discussion with the librarian. I lurked in the corner trying to sip my coffee without anyone noticing since I'd chosen to ignore the no food or drinks sign on the front door.

Licking my lips, I tossed my empty cup in the trash, and Dylan waved me over to him. "What's up?"

He led me to a quiet table toward the back of the library. "We found some information on Henry Willis on Google, but it's from years ago. He's probably dead, but we couldn't find an obituary."

Great. What good would a dead man do us? It's not like it was his ghost we were seeing. But Dylan seemed undeterred.

"The librarian said that I've been using the right databases, but a lot of the local papers still haven't been scanned in yet. Local archivists are still collecting newspapers from folks who find them in their attics and in boxes when their relatives pass."

"Okay. So, why are we still here?"

He pulled out a chair for me, then sat in the one beside it. "Because there are a few things that have been scanned. The librarian's gone to get a mobile microfilm viewer for us and a box of microfilm spools that will have articles and obituaries from the local papers. Not the really old ones. We've probably already found what we can find there until the archivists scan more in. But everything from the *Harland Observer* has been catalogued on microfilm since 1978."

"Meaning?"

"Meaning if Henry Willis died in this area after 1978, we should be able to find out more about him."

A petite librarian wheeled a cart toward us with a microfilm viewer and a large box. "Here you go," she said. "All of the *Harland Observer* records from 1978 until last year. They'll have this year done by February of next year. So you'll have to come back for those records if you need them. Or you can try online. They do publish some of their articles electronically."

"Thank you, ma'am." Dylan took the box from the librarian with a smile befitting a southern gentleman.

"Do you need help operating the viewer?" She gestured to the plastic black box with a big screen.

"No, thank you. I've used one before." Of course he had. Dylan took the box from her with a confident grin that was sure to win her over. No wonder he got all As; he knew how to charm the pants off a librarian and probably teachers, too. Not that he'd ever do it on purpose. I didn't think he would, anyway.

"Okay, well let me know if you kids need anything." With the flick of a smile, the librarian disappeared into the labyrinth of bookshelves.

Dylan set the box on the table and removed the lid. Each microfilm reel was labeled by year. Dylan poked through the box. "Now when could Mr. Willis have died?"

"Too bad Hunter didn't tell us that," I snapped, instantly feeling guilty for being annoyed with dead Hunter and his lack of information.

"Right. Well, let's go back twenty years and work our way up. If we don't find anything, we can go back further."

"What if he didn't even die in Harland?" I asked, worried about new research leading to nothing more than weird questions.

"The librarian found articles that showed he was involved in town about twenty years ago. And people who settle here don't leave often."

Of course they don't. They got stuck here just like me. A dead-end life in a dead-end town. Maybe that's why I didn't hate Daddy for leaving. He'd gotten away. He just forgot to take me with him. And that made me sad. I really thought he'd loved me.

"I doubt he moved." Dylan shrugged. "Besides, we've got to start somewhere."

Ugh. This was going to take a while. I scooted my still-bruised bottom back in my wooden library chair, wishing I had ordered a venti instead of a tall at Starbucks. And wishing I had taken ibuprofen before I'd left home. The cuts from the accident were healing, but the aches and pains and bruises were taking their sweet time, which was evident by the purple and blue-green skin on my face, backside, and arms. I clutched Hunter's bag close and tried to forget the pain.

Dylan loaded each microfilm reel on the viewer, turning the handle to spool through the films. The large screen magnifying the images, he flew through old newspapers, scanning the obituary sections. I read over his shoulder at first, then got bored after about the fiftieth obituary and zoned out.

After what seemed like an hour, Dylan stopped. "Here." His voice hitched with excitement. "I think I found it."

I twisted a crick out of my neck and leaned forward to look.

A black-and-white photo of a thin-haired, wrinkly white man stared back at me.

Northeast Harrison County—Henry A. Willis, 98 of Harland, Texas was born January 15, 1902, in Crossly, Texas, and passed away November 10, 2000, at home in Harland. He was a member of the Snake Creek Masonic Lodge and the Bayside Shrine Club.

He began his career in law enforcement in 1930 with the Texas Liquor Control Board and retired in 1972 after serving over 40 years as Harrison County Constable.

Henry Willis was preceded in death by his parents, Eugene and Hellen Willis; and wife, Margaret A. Willis. He is survived by his children Mary Willis Olson of Harland, Texas, Frank Willis of Harland, Texas, and Constance Willis Johnson of Essex, Connecticut, and his grandchildren Henry Willis Jr., Frank Willis Jr., Patricia Olson, Betty Johnson, Sandra Johnson and Raymond Johnson. And eleven great-grandchildren.

A heavy sense of disappointment settled in my chest. Great. Our one lead was likely a ghost, too. "Okay. What good will Henry Willis do us when he's been dead for years?"

Dylan looked back at the obituary. "Well, we know more about him now. Maybe one of his kids will know something."

"If they're still alive. This obituary is years old." I snapped a picture of the obituary with my phone.

Dylan kept reading and he took a quick inhale. "Hey, look at this. The funeral was held at St. Phillip's."

"Really?" I shoved past his shoulder to have a closer look. It was the same church where Keisha and Hunter'd had their funerals. "Do you think Father Alvarez might know something?"

"I don't know how long he's been there, but it's worth a shot."

"Then let's go." The sooner we could find out whatever it was Hunter wanted us to know, the sooner all of this would be behind us.

———

FATHER ALVAREZ WAS in his office, his laptop illuminating his face. Dylan knocked on his open office door, and the father looked up. "Dylan. Kaitlyn." He smiled, took off his reading glasses, and set them beside the computer. "It's good to see you both." He rose and gestured to the chairs in front of his desk. "Please, come in."

We took our seats, and my stomach somersaulted like I'd just been dropped about fifty feet on some carnival roller-coaster ride. I hadn't wanted to come back here to talk about ghosts and demons with a man who thought all

I had were post-traumatic emotional problems. Yet here I was, feeling like I was about to give a confession.

The father looked at me, concern clear in his creased brow. "How are you, Kaitlyn? Any better?"

I tossed my head to the side in a half shrug. "The cuts and bruises are healing." *Just not the ones you can't see.*

He smiled a deep, knowing smile. One that said he knew there was way more going on with me than a few cuts and bruises. He closed the lid of his laptop and stared at us. "So, how can I help you today?"

"We've been doing some research." Dylan pulled the folded notes he'd taken on the Henry Willis obituary from the pocket of his khaki cargo shorts. "Were you here back in 2000 when Henry Willis died? It says the service was held at this church."

Father Alvarez looked from Dylan to me and back again. "I wasn't. I came here five years ago. But I know of him. Some of Mr. Willis's family have attended the church for years. Why do you ask about him?"

"It's just a name we—found," Dylan started, then faltered.

So I charged on, my fingers toying nervously with the strap to my bag. Dylan had no idea the good father had already told me about the Catholic exorcism hotline. With everything that'd been happening to us, I hadn't even thought to tell him. And, if I was honest with myself, I didn't want Dylan getting too close. Whether I liked kissing him or not, I sure wasn't going to let anyone get as close to me as Hunter'd been. "We think he's related to the tree and what happens out there, but we're not sure how."

Father Alvarez visibly relaxed. "So you still think there's something supernatural happening?" His voice wasn't condescending, but I knew he didn't believe us. I felt like I was back in elementary school and a teacher was asking me about a story I'd made up to cover a lie. "I've been here nearly five years and have heard rumors of hauntings, but nothing has ever been proven. It's calm here. Quiet," he said in a whisper that said he'd like to keep it that way.

"Please." My voice was way more desperate than I wanted it to sound. "It doesn't matter if you believe us. Just tell us what you know about him. It will help us . . . work through this," I tried to swallow my words, hating that I was half-lying to a priest. Who was I kidding? I was never going to work through any of this. Not my daddy leaving. Not my mama's drinking. Not Hunter and Keisha dying. Not now. Not ever.

Palms up, Father Alvarez shrugged. "I don't know much about him."

Dylan's shoulders slumped, but I kept pressing. "Then what about his children? Surely one of them came to church here? You said yourself that some of his family came here for years."

"Certainly. His daughter Mary Olson was a member of our congregation for years. She came every Sunday. She passed away last year, but her daughter Patricia still attends service every week."

Dylan's lips twitched into a thin smile, and I felt the first hint of hope I'd had in a week. "Can we get her address?"

Father Alvarez's eyes twitched nervously from me to Dylan, then down to the pencil he twiddled in his fingers. "I'm not comfortable sharing the information of my congregation."

"Please," I nearly begged. He had to help us.

He tapped the pencil against his desk, before stabbing it back into a pencil-filled cup. "Now I don't want you kids getting into mischief and bothering people."

I glared and pressed my lips tight, holding back the sass I wanted to dish out at him. Him of all people, who worked for a church that actually believed in demons and possession. But I wasn't gonna go there. Not now. Not after how he'd been last time. I didn't need another crucifix.

He held up his finger, seeming to sense I had something to say to him. "But if you were to visit that little antique store down on Farm Road 1960, you might run into her there." He smiled like he'd given us the winning lotto numbers.

I exhaled, glad I'd kept my trap shut. "The one with the cute front porch?" I'd always wanted to go in there, but never had any money to spend—so hadn't bothered.

"That's the one."

———

THE OLD ANTIQUE POST was less than a ten-minute drive from the church. We parked in the small gravel lot that was empty except for a rusty, old pickup truck. We hopped out and walked onto the front porch, past a wooden Uncle Sam yard decoration and a camouflage-colored wagon, probably a toy some bubba had gotten his son for Christmas in hopes he'd grow up to be a redneck, just like his daddy. We passed a set of peeling wicker chairs and pushed open the front door to the sound of a clanging cow bell and the smell of age and dust.

A woman with sun-freckled skin worked the counter, her graying dark hair pulled back in a knot behind her head. "Welcome to the Post," she greeted us, smiling.

Dylan smiled in return. "Thank you, ma'am."

"Help you with something?" Her accent was very heavy and very local.

"Actually . . ." He sauntered up to the counter. Man, he

could turn on the charm just like Hunter. Not that I'd ever really noticed before today. I'd always thought he was kind of dumb with girls. But like my daddy'd always said, there's two sides to every coin. "We'd like to talk to Patricia Olson," he said. "We're doing some research for a summer history project."

"Well, you done found her." The gap between her front teeth was wide, her smile wider. "I'm Patricia."

I stared. Could Patricia somehow be related to Agatha Archer? Is that why Hunter'd given us Mr. Willis's name?

"What kind of history project you working on?" She wiped down the counter with a dirt-gray rag.

"It's local history. About that old oak tree out on Gravel Hill Road."

Patricia froze. Her gaze slowly rose to Dylan's face, then shifted over to mine. She studied our faces for a moment before speaking. "You two are the kids from that car accident out there, aren't ya?"

A shiver crawled its way up my arms like a roach. It wasn't just how she said it, but how she looked at me. Her mocha-brown eyes bore into mine.

"Yes, ma'am," Dylan said with no hint of fear in his voice.

She sighed, came around from behind the counter, and flipped the store sign to *Closed*. "I figured one day someone else would come asking. No one's been here pokin' around since Old Joe. Took a lot longer than I imagined. My granddaddy always thought someone'd come during his lifetime." She shook her head and twirled the rag around her finger. "I'm sorry about your friends losing their lives in that accident. Real sorry. I've been prayin' for them and for you."

Yeah. Prayers. A lot of good that seemed to do them or us. "What do you know about it?" I asked. Could she have known there was something happening at the old tree this whole time and done nothing? I pressed down the anger threatening to spill out in words I knew I'd regret.

She walked past the counter toward the back of the store. "My granddaddy kept records. And so have I. I've got something that might help answer some of your questions." She disappeared into a back room, leaving me and Dylan staring at each other.

"I never see her in town," I said quietly. "I don't remember seeing her at the funeral. So, how'd she know we're the kids from the accident?"

"She probably saw the newspaper article. We made the front page. Nearly everyone in Harland knows about it."

"True enough. Or maybe she knows something else. Maybe she has all along. Maybe she could've stopped what happened?" My voice cracked, but I tried to keep it down. If she knew and could've stopped that accident, then I swear I'd never forgive her.

A few minutes later Patricia came back with a tattered, dusty box. She nodded for us to join her at an antique oak table where she placed it. She removed the lid and took out a leather-bound, brown-skinned journal.

"This here was my granddaddy's. He kept it since he was a young man. He said it was important. He said Mama and I needed to know about her." She flipped the book open to the beginning. "Mind you, not all of the kids knew about my grandma. My real grandma. Only *her* kids. Only Mama an' me."

Her kids? "Who was your grandma?" I almost didn't want to ask even though I was pretty dang sure I knew the answer.

She looked at us then, her eyes sad, almost pitying. "I think you know, darlin', if you're here asking about my granddaddy." She sighed and slipped a worn black-and-white photograph from the back of the journal and handed it to me and Dylan. "Agatha Archer, of course."

Staring back at me was a woman. The same woman I'd seen staring out of Dylan's eyes when he was possessed. But she wasn't angry in the picture. She was young and graceful with a sweet face, full lips, and a friendly smile. She wore a long, dark skirt and floral print blouse, and leaned lightly against an old-fashioned black pickup truck.

Shivers shot down my legs and over my arms like a horde of spiders on the loose. "Agatha Archer." I barely recognized my own voice. "And a black pickup truck."

My gaze slid over to Dylan and he took the picture from me.

"Yep." Patricia peered at the woman in the old photo. "The way my mama told it, my granddaddy loved that truck near as much as my grandma."

Patricia took the photo from Dylan. "Beautiful, wasn't she? My grandma. Never met her, mind you. She died when my mama was near a year old. Poor woman never even got a chance to hold her baby."

"What do you mean?" Dylan asked, his voice quavering slightly.

She slid the journal toward us. She pointed to a page she'd marked "1 of 2." "Read these," she said. "Come find me when you're finished, and I'll tell you what else I know."

Dylan and I sat shoulder-to-shoulder, the old journal between us. A little, flappy butterfly feeling tickled me in my belly. Anxiety? Excitement? Fear? I couldn't tell . . . but I hoped we were finally about to get some answers.

SEPTEMBER 20, 1926

It's been less than six months since my beautiful daughter, Mary, was born. Our daughter. Agatha's and mine. Agatha screamed and cried when they took the infant away. My daddy said Agatha wasn't good enough for me. Not good enough for us. A poor, single woman with no mama or daddy to look after her. It wasn't true, of course. Agatha was poor, but she was more than good enough for me. She was the best person I've ever met. I think he said what he did on account of his being the mayor and her having no money or family.

Then Daddy called her a witch. It was no good after that. Then Preacher Mellberg got involved. He said the mayor's son should never be involved with a poor, filthy witch. He said it wasn't natural. He said that no man should ever have a child with a witch-woman— unmarried at that. I knew they'd never let me marry Agatha, but I never expected they'd do what they did.

The preacher said he couldn't rightly kill the child, but that my name would be better preserved by removing her from town. At first I didn't know where they sent her, but I meant to find out. For Agatha's sake and the child's. But Agatha changed when they took Mary away. She said I was just as no good as the rest of the folks in town. She said I let them take her baby. She cursed and spat and wouldn't have me no more after that. I told her I loved her. I told her I'd always love her, even if the town called her a witch. I told her I'd find our baby. But she didn't believe me. She said she needed help. Powerful help. Not mine.

Well, I reckon she got lost trying to find it. I saw her today near the Piggly Wiggly. She's gone half-mad, for certain. Her hair was flailing wild and stuck full of twigs and leaves. Her eyes crazed. She said witchcraft was the only way she could make amends. She looked frightful. My hands are still shaking. She said she could make a deal now. A deal with the devil himself. She said if I weren't the baby's daddy she'd curse me, too. But the baby needed her daddy. Me and my kin. She said she'd protect her kin. But she promised she'd curse the other folks in town.

. . .

WE READ the second entry Patricia had marked.

SEPTEMBER 23, 1926

I don't know that I believe in witchcraft or curses. But I know the townsfolk do. Well, if they didn't before, they do now. They found out Agatha's been having rituals out by the old oak. The one near Agatha's house in Baker's Field. She's been dancing naked and carrying on beneath the moon. Howling and crying out to the devil himself. Calling for revenge. She never did that when I knew her. Never. I think Preacher Mellberg and my daddy drove her to it. Seems they turned her into the very thing they accused her of being.

Preacher Mellberg said there's no having it. He just came and told me now. He said he couldn't tell me before on account of my unnatural relations with Agatha. He said I might've tried to stop them.

God forgive me, but I would have. Witch or no witch. Devil or no devil, God could've decided about Agatha. But the preacher did it for Him. Preacher Mellberg looked me right in the eye and told me he was working for God. He said that's why they took Agatha and strung her up from that old oak last night. He told her she'd never see her child again. Then they killed her. They killed my Agatha.

I went to the oak this morning. I can't even begin to write what I saw. I took her body down and buried her safe and sound. That was the least I could do for her. I'm half surprised I'm not hanging from a tree myself at their hands. But it's done now. And I pray she's at peace.

Now I'm going to find Mary. I'm going to find our daughter. I'm going to make sure she knows who her mama was. I'm going to do right by Agatha if it's the last thing I do.

DYLAN CLOSED THE LEATHER JOURNAL, leaned back in the rickety antique chair, and rubbed his eyes. "Wow."

Wow was right. That poor woman had had her baby taken from her as soon as it was born, then been lynched for witchcraft. I couldn't blame her for being mad. I'd have been mad, too. I had no idea the roots of hate pierced so deep in our town. No idea at all. Maybe that's why Keisha was so angry. If Agatha had told her what happened to her —how she'd been betrayed by a man. Killed by men. Well, maybe Keisha was seeing a bit of herself in Agatha and a bit of Dylan in Mr. Willis. Maybe Keisha was seeing the folks in town in me.

Sorrow welled in my chest. Not just for my losing Hunter and Keisha, but for them losing their lives. For Agatha losing her baby and her life, too. It was all so unfair and cruel and wrong.

I pulled the journal over to me and reopened it, skimming the pages after Mr. Willis's September 23, 1926, entry, but there was no more mention of Agatha. He went on about his search for Mary, and about finding her when she was three. Henry got married eventually, and they adopted Mary from the orphan home she was in. His wife never knew the girl was his. She just took pity on a little orphan child and gave her a home. That must've given Henry some sense of peace for the part he'd played in Agatha's life. And death. But it sure didn't seem to have helped poor Agatha Archer find peace.

"So." Dylan pulled me out of my thoughts. "If Agatha really did turn to witchcraft to curse the town for taking her baby away, then maybe she did make some sort of deal with a demon. Maybe people getting killed and trapped out at that tree are all part of some curse."

"Ya'll finished reading?" Patricia came in, the gray rag wrung tight in her hands.

I nodded. "So you knew she was a witch this whole time?"

Patricia frowned. "My granddaddy never believed in witchcraft. He said my grandma was a good woman. He said she went crazy after my mama was taken from her. So, no. I don't know that I do believe in witchcraft or that my grandma was a witch. Maybe her spirit's still out at that tree. Maybe she's so angry people are getting killed out there on account o' her, but I don't know about witchcraft."

"Didn't you ever think it was strange that there've been so many accidents by that tree? Didn't your grandfather?"

Patricia tossed the rag into a bucket with a sigh and heaved herself into a nearby chair. "My granddaddy never got over my grandma's death. Not really. It's why he became a man of the law. He said the minister who hanged her, that Preacher Mellberg, was really just a part of the KKK. He said there were lots of white folks in town who'd believed in lynching black folks no matter what'd they'd done. Apparently, they lynched some white folks, too. I guess my grandma was one of 'em. He wanted to stop them KKK from hanging folks. Still, he had his own fears and prejudices. He didn't tell me and Mama about Agatha until my gram—his wife, Ellen—died. He hadn't wanted her to know he'd had a child with another woman. A woman accused of witchcraft at that."

So even after trying to make amends for the preacher kidnapping his child out of her mother's arms and for Agatha's death, Henry Willis was never willing to admit to his wife he'd had a child with a witch-woman. Even in his grief, he kept his past a secret. Maybe Henry Willis had loved Agatha. Maybe more than anyone ever knew.

I had a whole new level of respect for Dylan and Keisha. Keisha wouldn't have been lynched for dating Dylan, but it sure must've been hard. Hard for them both. Especially with Dylan's pig of a father. I'd been so ignorant. No one had judged me for having a black best friend —but, obviously, there was still a whole lot of judging going on between white folks and black ones, rich ones and poor ones.

Patricia shook her head and nibbled her bottom lip. "Ain't none of it right or fair, but I don't rightly know about witchcraft. Still, I do know what some of the old folks in town have whispered for years."

"What's that?" A rock formed in my throat, threatening to choke out my air.

"None of the young 'uns today believe 'em. Not at all. But those old codgers still gossip. Not right to my face, mind you, mostly whispers amongst each other. They said my grandma made a deal with a demon." Patricia shrugged, then crossed herself. "I'm Catholic. I go to church. I believe in God. Demons are real, but I don't know what my grandma had to do with them. Likely or not she did it, I can't say. But there's no reason you kids or anyone else should go on getting hurt or dying from some old superstition. All those old fools who did the hanging are long dead anyhow, and the gossipy geezers left talking about it will soon be gone to join 'em."

"Well, did the old geezers say anything else?" Dylan asked. "Anything more—specific—about the demon?"

"Sure. Right before he went an' tried to cut down that tree, Old Joe came in here ranting and raving at me like a madman. He said my grandma'd been a witch, and that she'd made a deal with some demon. He said she'd cursed us all."

"Did he happen to say the demon's name?" Dylan's face had gone deathly pale at the confirmation we were hearing.

Patricia looked up at us then, her voice shaky. "He sure did. Old Joe said the demon's name was Alastor."

CHAPTER 10

"OH. MY. GOD. A DEMON. THERE'S REALLY A FREAKING demon!" Ghosts were one thing. And witches, not so good, but still human. But demons? I'd been willing to accept the possibility when we read about them, but if they were real? Like, really real? I bounced my feet against the floorboard so hard and fast that my knees nearly knocked into my chin. Thank God I wasn't driving or I'd have swerved off the road and gone right into a muddy ditch by now. "What the hell are we gonna do?"

Dylan gripped the wheel so tight his knuckles were extra white. "There's only one thing I can think we should do."

"And what's that?" I snorted, watching the trees pass by the window a little too fast. "An' slow down. We don't need to be in another accident."

The car slowed slightly and Dylan loosened his grip on the wheel. "We need to go back and see Father Alvarez again. He's a Catholic priest. If anyone will know what to do about a demon, it'll be him."

My stomach hitched and twisted itself into a great big knot. "I don't know if he'll believe us."

Dylan gave me a quick sideways glance, then looked back at the road. "He's a Catholic priest. Of course he'll believe us."

At the church, we found Father Alvarez at his desk like he'd been earlier—his laptop churning and several religious books lying about. Dylan knocked on his open office door, and Father Alvarez looked up.

"Kaitlyn. Dylan." He nodded to us. "Did you have an opportunity to speak with Patricia?"

"We did." Dylan went in and sat in one of the empty chairs facing the father.

"Good. I hope that brought you some peace?" His question hung in the air like a dank fog that lingered in December—the kind that rolls in off the lake and coats the air so thick you can't see a foot in front of your face.

"Actually," Dylan said. "Meeting Patricia gave us more questions—"

"Oh." Father Alvarez looked down at his computer and sighed. "Did she tell you they're just rumors?"

"Yes," I said, sliding into the chair beside Dylan, holding my bag on my lap. "But it also gave us confirmation."

He looked up at us, eyes weary. "Confirmation?"

"You remember what I told you? About how we'd seen Hunter and Kaitlyn?"

"You told him?" Dylan's eyes shot open nearly as wide as his mouth. "Why didn't you tell me?"

"It didn't make a difference at the time," I huffed, and pulled the crucifix out of my messenger bag. "He gave me this and told me he hoped I'd feel better."

"How could you not have told me? After everything we've been through together?" Dylan ran his hands through his hair, his face creased with betrayal.

"I'm sorry . . . II don't know. I didn't really think he

could help with ghosts." I shook the crucifix in front of him. "All he did was give me a necklace and say, 'God bless you.'" I could see the father cringe, but so what? It was the truth. "So there was no point telling you, was there?"

"There was no point?" Dylan's face was red. The only time I'd ever seen him this mad was when Hunter wrecked Dylan's new car after driving too fast out on Route 20.

"No, it didn't occur to me to tell you I came here in the middle of the night after your girlfriend attacked me." I glared at him. It wasn't like I had to tell him every move I made. Who'd he think he was, anyway? My mother? My boyfriend? Ugh.

"Kaitlyn. Dylan." Father Alvarez's voice was soft and patient with an underlying edge that said I'm-tired-of-dealing-with-other-people's-problems. "Please, stop arguing. One of the reasons I came to this town was because it's calm and quiet and small. When I was in Chicago . . ." He stopped, weighing his words. "Let's just say that most cases of reported hauntings or possession end up being people with emotional issues. Less than one percent of all the calls to the exorcism hotline are anything more than psychiatric problems."

"There's an exorcism hotline?" Dylan looked so surprised, I nearly laughed. And I would have if I wasn't still ticked off at him.

"Apparently," I snorted, then turned straight back to Father Alvarez, pretending Dylan wasn't pissed at me, too. "But there is a one percent chance that it's not because both of us are emotionally damaged from the accident that we're seeing things, right?"

Father Alvarez frowned, but didn't argue.

I pulled out Henry Willis's journal, thankful Patricia had let us borrow it, with a promise it would be returned. "Listen to this." I opened the book and read to the father about Agatha Archer and how the townspeople had taken her baby and then later hanged her for witchcraft. When I finished, I closed the book. "And Patricia said for years that some of the old folks in town have been saying Agatha made a deal with a demon."

"They're old and superstitious. They need something to talk about. Nothing more." Father Alvarez sounded like he was trying to convince himself that everything he said was true.

"Did you know Old Joe?"

"I didn't. I knew of him, but we never met. I was sorry to hear of his passing."

"He was old and maybe a little crazy, but people in town respected him. He wasn't a gossip." I leaned forward to make sure Father Alvarez was really listening to what I had to say. "And do you know what Old Joe told Patricia right before he went and died out there?"

Father Alvarez gave a little shake of his head.

"He said Agatha made a deal with a demon named Alastor."

All the color leaked right out of Father Alvarez's face when I said that. I must've hit a nerve. "*Dios* be with us." He looked at me, a tiny gleam of sweat glistening on his forehead. "Are you certain? That was the name?"

"You know of him?" I asked casually as if the thought of a real freakin' demon didn't scare the crap out of me, and then tucked the journal back in my bag for safe-keeping.

Father Alvarez crossed himself, rose unsteadily to his feet, then turned to one of his loaded bookshelves. "If . . . and it is a big if . . . but if what Joe said is true, then . . ." He scanned the titles with his fingertip, stopping on a dark book bound in leather and embossed with gold. He pulled it from the shelf, sat back down, and opened it. After flipping a few pages, he stopped and looked up at us, fear plain on his face. "I'd hoped the accidents and rumors out there were nothing more than local superstition. No one ever had any real evidence. And no one's died there since I've been here."

"You mean until Hunter and Keisha died," I spat, the heat rising in my cheeks. We hadn't been chased by some old folk superstition any more than Hunter and Keisha had been killed by it.

The father let out a long sigh. "Yes. Since I've been here no one has died out that way until your accident." His words came out in a harsh whisper, and his eyes devoured the page of the book in front of him until he finally looked up at us. "According to the Church, Alastor is a vengeance demon. Very cruel and very deadly." He set the book before us, its page opened to a medieval-looking drawing of a creature with scales and fangs and massive horns. "He's linked with possession," he said slowly. "So if what you're telling me is true"

"Of course it's true," I nearly yelled at him, spit flying out and spattering his desk. "Why on God's good earth would we make it up?" Stupid thing to say. Lots of kids made stuff up to get attention, but I wasn't one of them. Still, I couldn't blame him. He probably heard all sorts of crazy stories. But he had to believe us. He had to. Ghosts were real. And, apparently, so were witches and demons. If we didn't do something, that witch and her demon would torment Hunter and Keisha, and then me and Dylan would be haunted for the rest of our lives . . . if they even let us live.

"I'm not trying to diminish your pain"

I gritted my teeth and pulled down my shirt collar so he could see the finger-mark bruises around my neck. "Oh, you're not diminishing anything. It's real, alright, Father. They're real. Do you see these?"

He nodded, pale lips pressed together, probably wondering if Mama'd had a go at me.

"These are not superstition. These are finger marks. Keisha's finger marks. She did this to me last night." His mouth opened slightly, but I pressed on. "Yes, Keisha. The dead girl." I pulled my collar back up. "Not my mama. Not Dylan."

Dylan sat up straight, nearly jumping out of his chair. "Hey"

I held up a hand to shush him. "I'm just saying. No one living is to blame. It's Keisha. And she's not too pleased about being dead and me hanging out with her boyfriend." I looked at Dylan, then back at the priest. "And if we don't do something about Agatha's spirit and that demon curse, then me and Dylan won't ever be free. None of us will."

Father Alvarez closed his eyes for a minute and murmured a prayer in Spanish, sweat beading around his forehead. When he opened his eyes, he looked scared to death, but sure about something. "I'll come with you to the tree. I need to be certain about what we're dealing with." He rose to his feet and collected a crucifix, a Bible, and a bottle marked with a gold cross. "I'll bless it, and we'll pray for any lingering spirits to cross over."

"Is it really that simple?" Dylan got to his feet and Father Alvarez handed him the bottle of holy water.

"We'll just have to see."

———

I RODE with Dylan out to the Devil's Tree, Father Alvarez trailing close behind in his blue Chevy truck along old Gravel Hill Road. I never imaged a Catholic priest, or any priest for that matter, driving a pickup truck. Then again, I'd never imagined a priest wearing cowboy boots either.

Not more than fifteen minutes later we all climbed out of our vehicles and stood staring at the Devil's Tree. It wasn't so scary in the daylight, but we hadn't broken out the Ouija board yet. Heck, Father Alvarez didn't even know we had the Ouija board with us. I hoped Dylan wouldn't mention it.

The father walked up close to the tree. Closer than I'd have felt safe. "Is that where Old Joe tried to cut it down?" He pointed at the deep hack marks in the tree bark near the base of the trunk.

I nodded, licking my cracked lips. "I think so."

"And this is where you took the photographs?" he asked Dylan, his faint Mexican accent more pronounced than I'd noticed before.

"It is."

"And Hunter went and peed around the backside," I added. The newspaper hadn't mentioned that part of our story. "That's when things really started to get weird."

"He urinated on the tree?" Father Alvarez looked like he'd gone and swallowed a lemon tart—whole.

I shrugged. "He had to go and thought it'd be funny, I guess."

Father Alvarez frowned, but removed his Bible and some notes from the satchel he carried over one shoulder, and then looked at Dylan. "Do you have the holy water?"

"I've got it here." Dylan pulled the small glass bottle from his pants pocket.

Father Alvarez pressed his lips into a nervous line. "Okay. I'm going to pray over the tree, and you sprinkle the holy water on it as I do. Kaitlyn, I need you to sprinkle salt."

"Right. Salt." I nervously scraped at a scab on my

knee, then jerked my hand away at the sight of fresh blood. That's just what I didn't need to be doing, ripping apart the pieces of me that were actually healing. But I needed something to keep my hands busy.

From his satchel, Father Alvarez removed a plastic sack of white crystals, which he handed to me. "This is blessed salt. As I pray, sprinkle it around the base of the tree."

I took the bag and shoved my hand inside, the small crystals rough and sharp against my fingertips. Okay, this was something I could do, especially if it would help send away a demon.

Father Alvarez whispered a prayer, then opened his Bible, tucking his notes between the pages. He began walking around the tree as he spoke. "We drive you from us, whoever you may be, unclean spirits, all satanic powers . . ."

The sky grew dark and thunder rumbled overhead. That same freaky wind that always seemed to spring up around the old oak started whipping my hair into my face. I wanted to bolt, but stuck my hand into the bag of blessed salt instead. It stuck to my fingers and wedged itself beneath my nails—but I pulled out a handful and tossed it at the tree. Boy, I sure hoped this worked.

Dylan tossed some holy water on the tree and Father Alvarez kept praying. "All infernal invaders, all wicked legions, assemblies, and sects."

The tree began to creak and moan. Not just a little moan like when the wind blows and makes the branches twist, but a deep, dark, terrible moan that seemed to come from inside the tree itself.

I saw Old Joe first. He hung from a limb, his body mangled and swollen and blue as if he'd just been dragged from the watery ravine where he died. He looked straight at me, his words gurgling out, creek water dribbling down his chin. "You kids shouldn'ta come . . . but nobody listens, do they?" His cloudy eyes swung over to Father Alvarez. "Nobody listens. Do they, Father?"

Mouth slack, Father Alvarez stuttered and took a step back.

That's when I spotted the bodies. Some were in old-timey clothes. A few were in new ones. Then I saw Hunter. His disfigured body lingered in the branches, swinging like a grotesque piñata, his neck broken and mouth hanging open. But he looked at me, his charred lips and face a mask of pain. "Help us, Kaitlyn. Help us."

Keisha's body appeared on a branch not too far from Hunter. Same thing. Broken and swinging, hanged from the neck. "It's your fault, Kaitlyn. We should never have come. It's all your fault we're here."

Hand back in the salt bag, I started crying. It wasn't my fault. I didn't want to come out to this stupid tree. I couldn't do this. I wouldn't. I turned to run, but came face-to-face with the wild-haired witch-woman. Her eyes were crazed and her neck broken.

"Just where do you think you're going?" She glared at me. "No one escapes my tree more than once." Agatha Archer may be dead, but she was still a witch. And she was pissed. Standing less than a foot in front of me, she made a hideous, rattling sound as her reeking breath billowed into my face. I gagged at the smell. It was something like sulfur and rotten meat.

Father Alvarez glanced at the ghosts, then went back to reading the notes in his Bible, his voice hurried and shaking and shrill. "In the Name and by the power of Our Lord Jesus Christ, may you be snatched away and driven from the Church of God and from the souls made to the image and likeness of God and redeemed by the Precious Blood of the Divine Lamb."

Hunter and Keisha and all of the other spirits wailed like they were being tortured. The sound of their cries rattled my bones and wormed its way into my soul. I dropped the salt bag and covered my ears.

The wind howled and thunder crashed.

Dylan grimaced in pain, but he didn't cover his ears. He kept going, tossing more holy water at the tree. Then Agatha was there . . . right next to him.

Before I could scream for him to watch out, she smacked his hand, making the holy water fall to the ground. It drained from the bottle and seeped into the earth like blood.

The spirits' screams intensified and the wind raged, but Father Alvarez kept reading. "Most cunning serpent, you shall no more dare to deceive the human race, persecute the Church, torment these children of God, and sift them as wheat—"

Everything fell silent.

It was almost like the eye of a great big hurricane was passing over. Even Father Alvarez stopped praying. We all looked up. Hunter and Keisha were gone. I didn't see Joe or Agatha. Only dark, empty, creaking branches.

Then Dylan collapsed to the ground and began thrashing around like he was having some sort of seizure. His eyes rolled back until they were nothing more than blue-veined whites, and a hoarse, raspy voice clawed its way out of his throat. "I'll sift *you* as wheat, Father."

Father Alvarez's lips peeled back in fear, hands trembling. "Our Father, who art in heaven . . ."

Dylan sat up, the sightless orbs that were his eyes gazing directly at Father Alvarez. And then he laughed, deep and vile and cruel. It was the most vicious laugh I'd ever heard, and a guttural, raspy not-Dylan voice came purring out. "You think you can dislodge me with *that*, you unclean man?"

Father Alvarez stopped mid-sentence, looking from me to whatever Dylan had become.

"You'd better be ready to face your own demons, Father, if you want to face me," he hissed. "Does the girl know she's trusted a priest who fled from the likes of me? She trusted one who fled from the writhing mass of humanity where demons thrive? She trusted a priest who has built his entire life on a lie?"

My legs screamed at me to run, but I was frozen in place with fear. Father Alvarez had run from a demon before? He'd built his life on a lie? "What's he talking about?" I barely heard my own words against the thumping of my wild heart.

The thing that was Dylan swung his head and looked at me, his face no longer Dylan's but some sort of hideous beast contorting Dylan's skin. His face like a mask from some terrifying Halloween carnival. The stench that rolled off of him was like the meat I'd forgotten in Hunter's truck one night last summer after work. Rank and rotten. Vomit burned its way up my throat, but I forced it back down.

"Ask the good father what the Catholic Church thinks about priests who prefer men, girl?"

"Stop!" Father Alvarez's voice cracked. "You're a demon of deceit and lies. Leave this boy at once."

Wait. What? Father Alvarez liked guys? But he's a Catholic priest . . .

The thing rose to its feet and ripped Dylan's shirt open, revealing his bare chest and lightly muscled abs. "Come now, Father. Tell us the truth about your desires." The thing inside Dylan slowly licked his lips and gave the father a wicked smile. "The desires you hide so well from your precious Church. The desires you even try to hide from yourself."

Father Alvarez was crying now. Not just a few tears, but rivers of them. He backed away from Dylan and looked back at me. "I'm sorry, Kaitlyn. I'm so sorry, but I can't—I can't do this." He tucked his Bible into his bag and headed for his Chevy.

"What do you mean you can't do it?" My voice hitched with hysteria and I screamed after him. "You can't leave us!"

Father Alvarez looked at me. His face filled with sorrow and shame, the priest turned and ran the last few steps, quickly leaping into his truck.

"Where are you going?" I shrieked.

"I'm sorry." Father Alvarez slammed the door of his cab and the engine roared to life, then he tore off down the gravel road leaving me alone to face the demon.

Dylan took a step closer to me, a nasty smile on his face. "It's just you and me now, girlie." He leaned closer. "Should I tell you what this boy thinks of you. Should I tell you what he wants to do with you." He ran his hand down the front of his jeans and grabbed his crotch. "So much unexpressed desire."

I looked away and started crying. This wasn't Dylan. He'd never do something like that—ever. "Dylan would never betray Hunter."

"Oh, he loved Hunter, true. He even cared about Keisha. But this boy would have taken you from his friend given the chance. He dated the black girl to be closer to you."

Was that true? Had Dylan really started dating Keisha to spend more time with me? Or was the demon just lying to upset me? My stomach twisted in nauseous knots. He was so close now I could feel his hot breath on my cheek, the stench of rotting eggs overpowering. I stepped back, but he grabbed my hands hard, nails digging into my skin.

Tears rolled down my cheeks. "Please. Let Dylan go. You don't need to do this. You've had your vengeance." I looked up at the tree, desperation seeping into my blood. "Agatha, if you're still here. Please, call off this demon!"

The demon pulled me close, his wet tongue slowly lapping the tears from my cheek. His breath soft and hot and smelled like the dumpster outside the local butcher's shop. "Agatha brought me here, but she can't send me back," he chuckled, a deep and gravelly sound that made my bones ache.

I took a deep breath and hoped that something I'd learned watching all those horror movies with Hunter and Dylan and Keisha might help me now. "In the name of Our Lord, Jesus Christ, I command you to leave Dylan's body."

He looked at me for a moment, his unseeing eyes wide. Then he tilted his head back and laughed, his eyes no longer white, but pale amber. "You helpless little fool. You really are nothing more than the white trash everyone thinks you are. You're stupid. Stupid. Stupid. Stupid. You're worth nothing more than the trailer you live in with that drunk mother who wishes you'd never been born. Why do you think your father left? His life was worthless. Just like you."

Fear and anger welled up in my throat. Fear that what he said was true. Anger to fight with every fiber of my being that it wasn't. I wasn't stupid and I wasn't nothing. I wasn't worthless. I couldn't be. I could do more than my mama. I could be more than her. I had to be.

He dropped my wrist then and shoved me to the ground.

Pain shot up my backside, making my already bruised

tailbone throb with agony. Tears blurred my vision and I leaned back my head, trying to get control of the pain in my ass and my heart. It was nearly dark as night despite it being the middle of the afternoon.

Dylan raised his hands in the air. Words I didn't understand began coming from his mouth. Probably Latin if I remembered the sound right from my freshman year.

At least he wasn't coming at me for the moment. This was the chance I needed. My eyes scoured the ground, searching for the bag of blessed salt I'd dropped. There. In the dirt, not more than three feet away. I lurched for the bag, scooped up a handful, and tossed it into Dylan's face, making sure that some landed in his open mouth.

He howled like an injured beast. Backing away from me, he clawed at his face, leaving a trail of bloody gouges down his cheeks. "It burns!"

The near-black sky began to lighten. I grabbed more salt and tossed it at Dylan. He screamed again and backed past the Devil's Tree.

His skin was red and welted where the salt had struck. He didn't look like Dylan at all anymore. More like some sort of deformed, demented version of himself.

He gave me a curled-lip smile. "It'll take more than a little salt to drive me from my host, girlie." Then he was gone like a gunshot into the woods. Only the lingering scents of sulfur and excrement were left where he'd stood.

Slowly, the rotten smell vanished and the sky cleared back to blue with white, puffy clouds. It was almost like nothing horrible had just happened. Almost.

"Dylan!" I screamed after him. The salt was supposed to chase the demon out, not chase Dylan away.

Doubt battled inside of me. Part of me wanted to run after him with my crucifix and salt. The other part wanted to bolt in the opposite direction—straight back to church to demand that Father Alvarez come back and help.

So, I sat for a minute—alone in the dirt and salt—waiting for my tears to stop. I could go after Dylan, but that didn't make much sense. If I did that, I'd be alone in the woods surrounded by wild animals and ghosts and a demon. Not a good idea.

Father Alvarez might refuse to help, but if we were at church, maybe he'd feel safer. Maybe I would, too. Then he could tell me if he'd seen demons before, and could give me something to help save Dylan. Something to put Hunter's and Keisha's souls to rest. Something to break the witch's curse. I'd do it on my own if I had to—even if he wouldn't come back to help. Dylan was alone out there and Hunter and Keisha were trapped. There wasn't anyone left to help them except me.

I backed away from the tree until I could feel the roadside gravel beneath my feet, then I turned and ran smack into Dylan's car. "Oh, crap." How was I supposed to get out of here? It'd take me hours to walk back to town.

Peering in through the driver's-side window, I spied Dylan's keys lying on the front seat. Oh, no. There's no way I was gonna drive. The last thing I wanted was to get behind the wheel of a car. First, I'd never driven a car in my life. Second, after the accident I'd sworn that the last place for me was in the driver's seat.

I closed my eyes and took a few deep breaths. In and out. In and out. An owl screeched overhead and my eyes popped open. Well, I couldn't stay out here. With this tree. Alone. I could climb in that car, start the ignition, and drive out of town. Just drive and drive and drive. How hard could it be? I was nearly eighteen. I could do it. I could drive. I could drive straight out of town and never look back.

Daddy said, *We've always got choices.* He'd made the choice to leave me and Mama. No. I wouldn't be like Daddy. I had a choice to make. And I needed to choose right. I could leave Dylan and Hunter and Keisha. Just leave them all like Daddy left me and Mama, and try to get on with my worthless life.

Or I could do something real. Something good. Maybe I could help them. Maybe I couldn't. But I sure as hell had to try.

So that left me with two choices. A long, hot, dusty walk back to church, which would take me nearly three hours. Or a fifteen-minute ride in Dylan's air-conditioned car without a license. I could break my feet or break the law. Well, shoot, under the circumstances, I hoped the cops would understand if I got caught.

I snorted back a laugh. Yeah, I could just imagine me trying to explain about Dylan being possessed by some demon and running off into the woods. They'd never believe me and I'd end up in juvie. That'd be the end of any dreams I'd ever had of getting out of this place and doing something more with my life.

Well, with Hunter dead, my dreams had gone and died along with him. So screw it. I'd do what I needed to do in the quickest way I knew how.

Grabbing the handle, I yanked open the car door. I'd drive the speed limit, but get myself back to Father Alvarez as fast as I could. There was no way I'd leave Dylan out there in the woods possessed by something evil, or leave Keisha and Hunter trapped with that witch. Whether I got out of this town or not didn't matter right now. What mattered was that I wouldn't be like my daddy. I was going to make the right choice. I wouldn't abandon the people I loved.

CHAPTER 11

ABOUT FIFTEEN MINUTES LATER I PULLED UP TO FATHER Alvarez's church. Driving turned out to be pretty easy.

Father Alvarez's pickup truck was alone in the parking lot. So, I walked straight inside to his office. His chair was empty, laptop closed. I can't say I was surprised after what we'd just witnessed.

I moved out to the hallway and peered up and down the hall in both directions, but heard nothing. I tried the sanctuary next. Maybe the good father had been as scared as he seemed and had gone in to pray.

That's when I heard a male voice echoing from the sanctuary. I opened one of the heavy wooden doors and immediately saw Father Alvarez kneeling, his head bowed.

"Father Alvarez." I interrupted his prayer, my voice echoing through the sanctuary, making me sound young and small and terrified.

His bent head shot up. He crossed himself, then stood and turned toward me, tears in his eyes. "Kaitlyn. I'm sorry. I—"

I waved away his apology. "It's okay, Father."

He walked up to me and held my hands in his own.

"No. It isn't." His voice dropped to a whisper. "But if they ever found out."

"What?" I searched his soulful face. Had what the demon said been true? "That you're gay?"

He winced and made a quiet shushing sound. He looked around the sanctuary as if someone would overhear us even though we were utterly alone.

Despite being pissed he'd gone and left me on my own with a demon, my heart ached for him. This wasn't easy for me, but it sure couldn't be easy for Father Alvarez either. It's not like any of us ran around chasing demons. And what that demon had said could really fry his world.

Father Alvarez took a seat in a pew and gestured for me to join him. "I've dedicated my whole adult life to God," he said in a whisper that told me this was not something he was comfortable sharing. "To something I love. It's something more important than me. Something bigger than anything I've ever known. But part of who I am doesn't fit with that something." He sighed, suddenly looking very tired and a little bit old.

It was sort of like my trailer upbringing didn't fit in with who I wanted to be either. But did that mean I shouldn't have more? Did that mean Father Alvarez shouldn't? Or Keisha? Should she have suffered Dylan's father and God knew who else just because of her skin color? What about Keisha's daddy? He was a good man and a great baker. The best. How much had he suffered because of the color of his skin? Even Agatha. She'd suffered because she was a poor, unmarried woman who had a child with the wrong man. The world was so unfair.

"II ran away from my last post in Chicago, Kaitlyn. I had my secret then. I suppose I've known for a long time. Even longer than I've been a minister, but I didn't admit it to myself for a very long time. No one else knows. No one but me. And, now, you." His voice quavered, drifted, and his eyes looked glassy, before refocusing on the crucifix above the altar. "There was another possession there. In Chicago. A real one. I was assisting with an exorcism and the demon called me out in front of my colleagues. I denied it, of course, and they believed it to be nothing more than the filth and lies of a demon." Father Alvarez looked at me then, sad and serious. "And they do lie, Kaitlyn. All demons lie. They twist their lies with the truth to confuse your mind and your heart. So you mustn't listen to him. You must be wary."

"But you did." My voice sounded hollow, fear and disappointment filling up the hole in my heart that was made when Hunter died.

He nodded. "I ran from the truth. From my truth. So I came here. Partly to escape the demon. Partly to escape what I didn't want the Church to know. I won't run again, Kaitlyn. But I'm still not ready to face that aspect of my nature in a public way. I don't want to give up my faith or this life, and the Church isn't ready to accept it." With a shake of his head, he gave a humorless chuckle. "How many demons are likely to be in a small Texas town?"

I guess one was enough. It sure was for me. I got it that Father Alvarez wasn't ready to face his truth. I really did. I'd run from Mr. Anderson when I should've stayed and punched him in his ugly mouth. But now, running wasn't an option for me, not anymore.

"Father." I squeezed his hands tight in mine. "I don't care if you're gay or not. Or why you ran before. That's not my business. And I don't plan on saying anything about it to anyone. Far as I can tell, you've spent your whole life trying to do what's right. Trying to help people and serve the Church, right?"

A tear slid down his cheek and into the graying stubble on his chin. "I have."

"Then there's no reason to stop doing that now, is there?" I weighed my thoughts and my words, wondering how I'd ended up trying to console a priest. "It seems to me like too many people judge other people for what they have or don't have, for what color they are or aren't, for who they are or aren't . . ."

Jaw clenched, he shook his head. "I've never acted on my thoughts. I've never—"

I held up my hand. "Like I said. That's not my business. But who am I to judge? It just seems like there aren't enough people in the world doing good. There're just too many of them out there trying to judge. And you're one of the good ones. So why on God's good earth would I go and try to stop you from doing good?"

"You won't say anything?" He looked at me, a look that asked if I could be trusted with a secret. With his secret. One that could utterly destroy his life.

"Nope. I've got no reason to. This town's better off with people like you in it." I stood up and tugged on his hand, pulling him toward his office. "Now why don't you come on and do what you're meant to be doing and help me send this demon back to hell."

"Wait." He yanked me to a stop with him. "There are things I'll need from my office. But if this is to be done properly, first I need to cleanse you."

"Cleanse me?" Oh, Lord. If he only knew all the cleansing that'd need to be done. I may be young, but I had more sins than a barn cat stuffed full of mice. And he thought he could cleanse me in an afternoon?

"I'm not ready to face a demon again, Kaitlyn. Not yet. Especially not after what happened today. You can't have any uncertainty—demons seize on that, thrive on it.

I'd be worse than no help. And with Dylan possessed by that creature, we don't have time to get the Catholic Church to approve a formal exorcism. You should have a priest perform the ritual, but under the circumstances, I'll make you as ready as possible."

"Okay." My stomach did a flip-flop. Was he really planning to cleanse me, then send me back to exorcise a demon? Alone? I stifled a laughing cry.

He led me to the altar and placed a deep purple shawl around his shoulders. "The Body and Blood of Jesus Christ are truly, really, and substantially present in the Eucharist. Do you believe in the Lord Jesus Christ? That He died for your sins and is your Savior?"

I nodded my head and gave a half shrug. "I guess. It's what my grandma used to tell me." When she was sober enough to talk without slurring. "But I've never really gone to church." And never Catholic church.

He took a little disc-shaped wafer with a cross from a small box near the altar and poured some red wine into a large golden goblet. "As long as you believe in your heart. That's what matters."

Did I believe? Really? I couldn't lie to myself. Not about this. Not if I was gonna head out there and try to get rid of a damn demon. Was God real? Jesus? A week ago I wouldn't have even thought about if I believed in anything supernatural. But now Hunter and Keisha were dead. I'd seen their ghosts. I'd seen the ghosts of Old Joe and Agatha Archer. And demons? The Catholic Church believed they were real. I'd seen one in Dylan. So, if demons were real, then I guess that meant angels and God were real, too. They had to be. I opened my heart, took a huge breath through my nose, and let it slowly out with my words. "I believe, Father."

"Then kneel." Father Alvarez gently pressed my

shoulders until I knelt before the altar, the massive crucifix with Jesus looking down at us. "Soul of Christ, sanctify this girl; Body of Christ, save her; Blood of Christ, inebriate her; Water from the side of Christ, wash her; Passion of Christ, strengthen her; O good Jesus, hear her; within Thy wounds, hide her; let her never be separated from Thee; from the evil one, deliver her; at the hour of my death, call her and bid her come to Thee, that with Thy saints, she may praise Thee forever and ever. Amen."

A ripple of energy flowed through me. A kind of tingly wave that made me light and giddy and hopeful all at the same time. If there was a God, which I now believed there was, then I'd just felt Him. "Whoa. That was some prayer."

He blessed a wafer and the wine, then gave me what he called the Eucharist, which I knew from TV as holy communion.

The bread, which he called "the body of Christ," was like wafer-thin cardboard. It was quickly followed by "the blood of Christ," which was tart wine. I swallowed the wine-flavored paper, and wondered how this would help protect me from a demon.

Father Alvarez smiled at me, then made the sign of the cross on my forehead with holy water.

"You're now ready to face the demon, Kaitlyn. But first, I need to get a few things that will help you."

―――――

FATHER ALVAREZ KNELT and unlocked a cabinet in the corner of his office that I hadn't really noticed before. It was made of dark wood and carved with crosses. He pulled out a small glass bottle and a bag of salt, then rummaged around for a minute, before pulling out a thin book. "Here it is."

The father stood up and opened the book. "This is a work by Father Amorth. For many years, he was the exorcist for the Diocese of Rome. He was also the founder and honorary president of the International Association of Exorcists. He's said to have exorcised over seventy thousand individuals in a twenty-five-year period." He read through a few pages, before stopping. "These are all prayers he used in exorcisms. Use the *Roman Ritual* and this one."

He handed me the book and I read the title of the page. "Prayer Against Every Evil," I said aloud, my voice shaking. "Okay. And you're sure this will work?"

Father Alvarez gave me a nod-shrug, which wasn't too comforting. "Only priests can perform true exorcisms, but you can say prayers of deliverance, which might work."

Might work. Great. I needed more assurance than that, but what choice did I have if I wanted to save Dylan and help Hunter and Keisha?

The father handed me a small glass bottle embossed with a golden cross similar to the one he'd given Dylan. "This is holy water from the Jordan River near the very spot where Jesus was baptized. And, this," he handed me the bag of salt. "This is salt from the Red Sea. It's been blessed by Israeli rabbis and Catholic priests. The demon will flee from both the water and the salt."

I put the bag of salt into my messenger bag and the bottle of holy water into my pocket, hoping all of it would make a difference. "Why didn't you bring all of this with you when we went to the tree to begin with?" I had a feeling I already knew the answer, but I had to ask anyway.

"As I told you, true demonic possessions are extremely rare. So I brought holy water and blessed salt, just not from

Jordan and Israel . . . Please understand, Kaitlyn, in my position I must explore every possible option first to ensure there isn't a medical or psychiatric condition causing the issue. The existence of ghosts is widely debated in the Catholic Church, and the presence of demons takes time to evaluate. But I know what I saw today . . . Still, there is no time for Church approval." He looked down before finally meeting my eyes. "I'm so sorry, Kaitlyn. I really didn't think it would be possession. I believed a simple blessing would be sufficient to end the pain and suffering that happened to you at that tree. I believed it would be enough to help restore you from the trauma you've endured."

"So you didn't really believe we'd been seeing ghosts? Not even a little bit?"

Father Alvarez gave me another half shrug. "I haven't seen any true possessions except for the one in Chicago. Even the Pope discourages exorcisms unless we're abso-lutely certain there is a demonic presence. As I said, most cases stem from emotional crises, not demons. Now I know it's real. Please forgive me."

I pulled my bag over my shoulder and tightened the strap. "Well, at least you believe me now." For what it was worth.

He let out a long sigh through his nose. "I do. Be careful about using the demon's name. Only use it to summon him if you must. Remember what I said, don't let any fear or uncertainty show. Demons can read your thoughts and feelings. They feed on negative emotions." He gestured to my hunter-green bag, now stuffed with exorcism goodies. "I've given you the tools you need to send the demon away. Just rest in your faith."

I didn't have much faith, but I nodded anyway. "I'll do

my best." I pulled Hunter's bag close to my body and tight-ened the strap. Ready for battle.

"God bless you, *hija*. I'll be praying for you."

I gave him a tight-lipped smile and nodded. "Thanks. I'll need it."

———

THE THOUGHT of Dylan with that demonic thing inside him sent shivers crawling along my arms and back. I sure hoped all this stuff Father Alvarez had given me would work because the sooner I could get that demon out of Dylan, the better. But I had to make one stop before I went back to the tree. I had an idea. Just a hunch, but I thought it might work. I had to see Patricia.

It took me over ten minutes—driving just under the speed limit—to get to the Old Antique Post from the church. I was getting the hang of this driving thing. Sort of. Next, I'd need to get a license.

I parked right out front next to the same rust-brown pickup truck that'd been there when Dylan and I'd come. I figured Patricia must be in.

The old cow bell clanged when I pushed open the front door. And Patricia was standing in the exact same place as last time, but this time she was making notes in a ledger. She looked up at me soon as the bell clanged and the door thudded closed behind me.

She shook her head slightly, then came out from around the counter. "You come to give me back my grand-daddy's journal?"

"Not yet. If you don't mind I'd like to keep it a little bit longer." I didn't know exactly what I needed, just that it had to be personal. Something to link Agatha to her family.

I'd gotten the idea when I'd filled Hunter's bag with everything Father Alvarez gave me.

Patricia looked over my shoulder toward the door, as if expecting someone else to come walking through. "Where's that cute friend of yours?"

I tugged the strap of my messenger bag snug against my shoulder, and hugged it to my queasy belly, a motion that was becoming a habit to make me feel more secure. "He's still out there . . ."

"In the woods?" Her nostrils shot open and she grabbed the counter, her short, chipped nails clinging to the edge to steady herself. "At the Devil's Tree?"

Tears I didn't even know I'd been holding in busted out of my eyes and ran in rivers down my cheeks. All the fear and anger and worry I'd held in with Father Alvarez came pouring out of me. I sucked back a sob and nodded.

In a split second, Patricia was there, her bony arms wrapped around me. "Come on now, sweet girl." She squeezed me tight, and I let myself go in her embrace. I couldn't remember the last time I'd had a hug like this. A good, solid, motherly hug. I just cried and cried and cried until there was a big wet patch on Patricia's shirt. "It'll be alright." She stroked my hair and patted my back like loving on me was the most natural thing in the world.

I let her hold me like that for a long time, letting the comfort of her arms ease my battered heart. I finally pulled away a bit and wiped snot away with the back of my hand, slick and wet and almost as disgusting as I felt. "I —don't—see—how," I gasped.

Patricia grabbed a box of tissues and handed it to me, then shoved a stool my way. "Sit yourself down right here and tell me what in tarnation's goin' on."

She pulled up another stool for herself and sat across from me and patted my knee encouragingly.

After several shuddering breaths, I calmed myself down and told Patricia everything that'd happened since we'd first been in to see her. I told her about what'd happened with Father Alvarez and the tree and Agatha and Dylan and the demon. Of course, I left out the part about Father Alvarez being gay or running from another demon like I'd promised I would. It didn't make a difference anyhow. I just told her he'd been right freaked out.

And I told her my idea. I needed something personal. Anything.

By the time I finished, Patricia was standing, wringing her hands and pacing. Back and forth. And back and forth. And back and forth. "I don't know. I don't know about any of this, child. I don't want to go messing about with nothing supernatural. Especially when my own preacher won't even go back to that tree." She crossed herself.

"Please," I nearly begged, but stopped myself. She was afraid, I could see that. And now I understood it. Fear is what kept that tree haunted all these years. And fear was what had made it haunted to begin with. Fear was a nasty thing. A powerful thing. Fear is what made people hate. Fear made people judge and make bad decisions.

Maybe they didn't hate Agatha for being poor. Maybe they were just afraid of what her poorness meant to them. Just like maybe folks didn't hate me for being from a trailer park. Maybe they were just afraid of what trailer park life was like or maybe they were afraid of living like that themselves. Same with Keisha. Maybe some white folks were just afraid of black folks because they looked different. Because they were judged based on the color of their skin. But I wasn't afraid of someone's color or of being poor. And my worst fear wasn't the tree anymore. Shoot, it wasn't even me being afraid I'd never get to leave this dead-end town and my loser life. No. My worst fear was that Dylan and Hunter and Keisha would be tormented for eternity by that demon.

"I didn't know where else to go. I just need something that'll help. Something besides all the stuff Father Alvarez gave me. I don't know what. It's just this feeling I've got." I looked up at her, my eyes stinging. "Isn't there anything you can do? Anything . . ."

She kept pacing back and forth, not bothering to look up at me. "I can't do nothing for ya. You'd best use what Father Alvarez has given you—or have him talk to the Church and wait for a priest. Or don't go back at all."

"I have to go back." I stood up, wringing the strap of my messenger bag until it cut into my palms. "I can't just leave Dylan out there. Or Hunter or Keisha either. I won't."

"Then stick with what Father Alvarez gave you, and surely the Lord will give you mercy." She crossed herself again, then stopped mid-pace and turned to look at me.

"What is it?" A whisper of hope tickled the pit of my stomach and fluttered into my chest.

She tapped her finger to her lips, then pointed it toward the back of the store. "There is something. Something I have that might just help you get through to my grandma."

———

FIVE MINUTES later Patricia had pulled a dusty old shoe box down from a backroom shelf. "Aside from his journals, this is the only other thing my granddaddy said I had to keep. There wasn't no question about it." She removed the lid, revealing a pasty-white rag doll with short brown braids poking up around its head in little knots. Its grotesque smiling face was sewn on and it wore a pink-

and-green plaid dress. "Keep my book and this dolly. Always keep them. That's what Granddaddy told me. Keep them close."

The doll's smile creeped me out about as much as its musty, decaying smell. "Whose was it?" My voice sounded strange and empty.

Patricia lovingly picked up the doll and stroked its braided head. "This here was my mama's doll. Grandma made it while she was pregnant with Mama." Her lips trembled. "Granddaddy got it from her house after they hanged her. He gave it to Mama soon as he got her back from the orphanage Preacher Mellberg put her in. Mama kept it from then on. It wasn't long before Mama died that she gave it to me. She told me it was the only thing she had of her mama's. It was the one thing that kept her connected to the most important person she'd ever lost."

Patricia stroked the doll's head one last time, then held it out to me.

I hesitated. I'd come here to find something personal, but could I really touch a doll made by the witch who'd made my life a living hell?

Patricia pushed the soft, demented-looking doll into my hands. "I don't have a daughter, only a couple of sons," she sniffed. "I was planning to give it to my niece . . ." She looked at the doll, then back at me. "But you need it. I know that now." She closed my fingers around the doll and held my hands in her own. "You give it to my grandma if you see her. You tell her about my mama. Tell her about Mary. Maybe it'll remind her she used to be a mama herself."

Something about the doll felt right in my hands. Old and dusty and fragile, but still right. Maybe Agatha and I weren't so different after all. Sure, we were from different times and different lives, but we'd both been poor and we'd both struggled to survive. We'd both lost people important to us. I'd lost my daddy, and, in a way, my mama, too. And Agatha had lost her only child. A pang of loneliness struck my heart. A twang of agony that must've been only a measure of what Agatha felt when she'd lost her daughter.

I tucked the rag doll safely into my messenger bag beside the book of prayer and blessed salt, and prayed Patricia was right. I prayed it would remind Agatha that she'd once been a mama. The kind of mama who'd do anything for her child. I prayed it would remind her of what it'd been like to love.

————

WHEN I PULLED up at the tree, the sky was turning a misty pinkish orange, and the sun was just settling back behind the trees. I climbed out of Dylan's car, being sure to leave the keys in the ignition in case I had to get away quick, then secured my messenger bag with all its anti-demon supplies over my shoulder and slammed the door shut. No need to be quiet or sneak around and pretend they didn't know I was coming. I was sure they knew: the demon, the witch, and any other spirit haunting the place.

Everything was calm. Calm and silent. Not a squirrel squeaking or a bird chirping. I took a deep breath of moist summer air and wished I could hear the sounds of crickets and cicadas. Usual summer sounds. As if in answer to my longing, the wind began to blow, tossing the leaves against each other in a raspy rustle, and whipping my hair into my face with a little slap, slap, slapping sensation 'til I tucked it behind my ear to make it behave.

The tree's dark arms reached up and out, black and bony against the dimming sky. I took a couple steps closer to the spot where Dylan had set up the Ouija board when the demon possessed him. I patted my pockets, feeling for the crucifix in my left and bottle of holy water in my right. Both were where I'd put them, ready and waiting. Next, I reached past the dolly and pulled the book of exorcism prayers from my bag and opened the salt so I could grab some quickly if I needed it.

As soon as I was ready, I faced the tree and took a deep breath of grassy summer air. "Dylan!" I called. "Dylan! Come on out. I came back for you."

I waited.

And waited some more.

The glowing ball of orange sun disappeared completely behind the sulking trees, and a nearly full moon rose into the sky. And still, no Dylan.

"Oh, come on." I scuffed the toe of my well-worn sneakers in the gravel and waited. Listening.

"Agatha. Keisha. Hunter," I yelled, my voice echoing through the darkening trees and foggy fields. "Some-body . . . anybody." My voice fell to a murmur on the breeze, then I sucked in a deep breath of humid summer air and let it all out in a single word.

"Alastor!" I hollered at the top of my lungs so that a few birds in a distant tree twittered up into the sky like tiny black pinpricks. Then there was nothing. No movement. No sound. Only hungry silence.

Kicking the gravel with my toe, and trying not to swear so I didn't undo the cleansing Father Alvarez had done on me, I trudged back to the car to get the one thing I hadn't wanted to bring out. The Ouija board.

It was lying on the floor of Dylan's backseat where we'd tossed it. I swallowed back the fear worming its way into my throat, grabbed the board, and headed back to the spot Dylan had set it up. I needed to call the supernatural, and this was the only way I knew I could do it that the spirits would obey.

I set my bag beside me and opened it so I could easily reach the salt. I tried to ignore the doll, which was staring back at me with dark, lifeless eyes. I shook away the goose bumps crawling up my arms, then opened the Ouija board and placed the planchette in its center. "This'd better work with just one person," I muttered. If not, I didn't know what I'd do. Maybe trek through the woods in search of a demonic Dylan? I shook my head wondering how on God's good earth I'd gotten myself into this mess, and then put my fingers over the planchette. This had to work.

As soon as I touched the pointer, a sort of zappy jolt shot through me, making my fingers tingle. The planchette began to move—slowly at first—in long, lazy, looping circles as if it was on a Sunday stroll. I didn't have Dylan's way with words, but I needed to say something. "Okay, spirits." I felt lame and stupid. The same kind of stupid I always felt when someone found out that I lived in a half-broken-down trailer at the edge of town.

Nope. I wasn't gonna go there. There was no point in letting a demon use my bad feelings or its twisted truth against me. "Hunter, are you there?" I reached out with my senses, hoping to feel him, but got nothing. The planchette kept looping round and round, not spelling anything. So, I took another breath and prepared myself for a whopping. "Keisha?"

That's when I saw it. A shadowy form beneath the tree, its eyes glinting in the moonlight. Her head was cocked at an awkward, unnatural angle, and she shuffled along the ground making a *scretch-scretch-scretch* sound in the gravelly dirt with the toes of her worn-out shoes.

My heart leapt from my chest to my chin and I grabbed a handful of salt.

Scretch. Scretch. Scretch.

Closer she came.

And closer still. She was wearing a long, pale dress with faded floral print. Not anything Keisha would've worn, which made sense since it wasn't Keisha.

"Agatha?" I croaked, all the bravery I'd felt in the safety of the church evaporating like the mist dancing and twisting around me.

"Why have you come back to my tree, girl? We let you live. That boy fought to let you live."

"What'd you mean? Hunter?"

"No, girl. Are you so thick-skulled you can't see what's right in front of you? Dylan. That boy's got a strong will. He tried to protect you. But Alastor has him now." She smiled, teeth hauntingly white in the moonlight.

"Being haunted isn't any way to live. You've got to stop this. Once and for all." I forced authority into my timid voice.

She crept to the edge of the Ouija board, not more than three feet from me, staring down at me like some little rodent she'd like as kill as set free. And she laughed. A hearty, cackling laugh that made my skin crawl.

"And why would I do that? Why, when this town took everything from me? Everything," she spat.

"It's taken a lot from me, too, Ms. Archer." I forced the words out, trying to reach some part of her that had once been alive. "This town made my daddy leave and took my mama, too." A surge of hopelessness engulfed me. I fought back tears, feeling myself go weak.

"And why should I care, little girl? It was the likes of you and your kin who brought me to ruin."

I looked her straight in the eyes, hoping, pleading for her to listen. "You're wrong, Ms. Archer. I'm not like that —even if some folks in this town are. I'm poor. Always have been. But things are starting to change. Little by little. Person by person. Keisha was my friend. A good one. And I couldn't care less about the color of her skin or what religion she practiced. I never cared about that. Ever. Sure, some white folks still think it matters. But there are also people who don't want to be associated with poor people like me, either. And why should that matter? Why should any of it matter? As long as no one's hurting anyone else— it shouldn't!" I shook my head, a sense of clarity coming into my mind that I hadn't had since—well, since ever.

"There are good people out there, Ms. Archer. And bad people. There are folks in between. Black and white, rich and poor. Some judge more than others. Some judge less. But I'm not one who decides if someone is good or bad, decent or not, based on what they have or on their religion or on the color of their skin." I took a deep breath, hoping I was getting through to her. "And as for why you should care? It's not on my account. It's for your granddaughter. She wants you to stop, too."

Agatha Archer froze when I said that and her evil eyes grew almost tender. "My granddaughter?"

I looked at her, then really looked at her. Her crazy hair was full of branches and leaves, her face streaked with graveyard dirt, her neck still raw from the noose. All these years of haunting and pain and misery and she didn't know. I realized it then. She had no idea what Henry Willis had done. She had no idea she still had family out there who loved her.

Tears ran down my cheeks and pity flooded my heart. Pity for Hunter and Keisha. Pity for me and Dylan. Pity for Ms. Archer and the whole mess that had become her life and her death. "Oh, Ms. Archer. I'm so sorry for all that happened to you. For those cruel, stupid people who took your daughter away and forbade Mr. Willis from marrying you. I'm sorry for all that's happened to all of us. There's so much you don't know."

She bit her lip in a way that almost made her look human. "Is Henry still alive?"

"Henry Willis?" My voice echoed in the darkness. Of course, she was asking about Henry Willis. "No, ma'am. He died several years back."

She clenched her teeth, her expression growing fierce again, and she took a step closer.

"But" I had to buy myself time. She had to hear me. Really hear me. It was my only chance to make things right. "He made sure you weren't forgotten. He found your daughter. He found Mary. He raised her himself and made sure she knew about you."

"Mary?" If ghosts could cry, she'd be doing it now. At least that's what her face looked like. "Mary's alive? And Henry raised her?"

I figured it wasn't any good to tell her that Henry'd been married and they'd adopted Mary from an orphanage and that Henry's wife never even knew Mary was his real child. That'd make her mad. So, I'd stick to what she needed to know. "Yes, ma'am. He raised her. But —" I didn't know if I should tell her Mary was dead or not . . . but she might demand to see her. So, I decided I'd better tell the truth. "It's been years since you passed, ma'am. Mary is in heaven now."

Her face grew dark at that, the rage in her eyes like boiling oil. But I rushed on. "She lived a long, happy life. She was married and had a child of her own. You have a granddaughter, Ms. Archer. Her name's Patricia. And she's still alive. And she has children. A couple sons, I think. So, you've got great-grandchildren. They know about you. They know you're their family. Henry made sure of it." I groped around in my bag and pulled out the doll. "And Patricia, your own granddaughter, gave me this."

I held the rag dolly out in front of me for Agatha to see. "She said you made it for her mama. For Mary. And Mr. Willis gave it to your daughter as soon as he found her."

Agatha dropped to her knees, then a sort of crackling, weeping sound escaped from the pit of her soul. "Patricia was my mama's name. My daughter." She gasped and reached out for the dolly. She was so close now I could feel the cold roiling off her like mist from the sea. "She got the dolly I made her." Tears sparkled on her cheeks. "My Mary named her child after my mama?"

"I suppose she did." I placed the old doll into Agatha's outstretched hands and recoiled from the chill that snaked its way up my arm.

"And Henry . . . he didn't give up on her?" She looked at me, her eyes wet and imploring. "He found her?"

I wanted to reach out to her, but didn't dare for fear she'd lash out at me. "Yes, ma'am. He did. He raised her and loved her with all his heart."

"And Patricia, my granddaughter." She said the word like it was a delicious piece of fruit, ripe and bursting. "My granddaughter wants me to stop."

"She wants the accidents and the killing to stop. And she wants you to be at peace." Maybe this would work. Maybe, after all these years of pain and desperation and longing, Agatha Archer would finally be at peace. Maybe she'd finally be free.

Agatha looked up at the stars for a long moment, holding the doll close to her heart. Finally, she rose to her feet, a look of calm resolution on her face. "Stand up, child, and prepare your water and your salt. Prepare your verses."

I cringed. How'd she know about what I'd brought?

As if reading my thoughts, she smiled. "You aren't the first to come and try to drive us away from here. But you are the first one who seems to understand. The first one who seems to care. You're the first one to tell me about my Mary." She stroked the doll's yarn hair. "The first one to tell me I have a granddaughter."

She was right. I did care. Losing my daddy had nearly crushed me. It'd crushed Mama, and I'd lost her, too. Sure, she was home every night, but drunk and mean and useless. She wasn't my mama anymore. Not really. Then I'd lost Hunter and Keisha. Of course, I cared. I understood. "How will this time be different?" My voice was nothing more than a hollow echo.

"You mean how will you not end up dead?" Amusement laced her voice, and she gave me a wicked, knowing grin. "Because I control Alastor. It was me who summoned him before my death. It is he who has killed and brought my curse on this town and its people. I can't send him back now that I'm a spirit. But I can help you do it."

Fear rippled through my veins, pounding into my soul with every pump of my heart. This woman—this witch— who controlled a demon stood right in front of me. And she had the power to help or kill.

She closed her eyes and murmured something under her breath, a prayer or a spell I couldn't tell. When she opened them again, she looked at peace. "I will summon him. I will do what I can to hold Alastor while you exorcise him from your friend. Then maybe I can finally rest." She looked at the doll and smiled. "Maybe I can finally be with my baby girl. My Mary."

CHAPTER 12

HANDS HELD HIGH IN THE AIR, THE RAG DOLL IN ONE hand, palm turned out with the other, Agatha faced the old oak and the woods beyond. She mumbled words I didn't understand, and the wind whipped and moaned, squealing around us like some unseen beast, tangling her mass of black hair like writhing snakes.

Unmoving, she stared into the darkness and called out. "Alastor. Alastor, I summon thee, demon. Return to our tree and serve me."

The wind beat against my face, howling through the branches. Great rumbles of thunder boomed in the air, and a terrible chill crept up and wrapped its arms around me.

Then suddenly everything went still. Dead still.

I stared into the cold, soundless dark, waiting.

There was nothing at first. No scamper of rabbit or chirp of frog. Not a sound.

"Prepare yourself, child." Agatha dropped one arm, the other still cradling the dolly to her chest, not bothering to look at me. "He's coming."

In a scuffle, I pulled the crucifix out of my left pocket

and lashed it around my wrist, then yanked the bottle of holy water from my right pocket and freed its lid. I slid the book of prayers from my messenger bag and opened it to the page I'd marked. It was the prayer of exorcism Father Alvarez suggested I use. Salt by my feet and at the ready, I stood and listened.

I still heard nothing. Nothing but the ache of dark silence. Then, softly at first, and growing louder, I began to hear a gentle rustling sound as if a rabbit were scrabbling in the underbrush, hunting for supper.

Then I saw him. His pale face glowed in the moonlight before his body appeared. It was Dylan, except it wasn't Dylan. The look on his face was cruel and hard, his mouth gnarled into a twisted smile in a gaunt face. Twigs and the remains of dead leaves poked out of straw-blond hair, dirt smudged his cheeks and arms and soiled his torn clothes.

"Dylan," I whimpered without meaning to.

Agatha spun around, baring her teeth like a snarling animal. "Let go of your fear, girl, or he'll take you before I can stop him." She was no longer a mama longing for her lost baby. She was a witch again. Angry and fierce and powerful. "Now focus on what you came here to do, and that boyfriend of yours might be set free."

Boyfriend? Was she talking about Hunter or Dylan? And I realized right then that I loved them both. Right or wrong. That's how it was. Hunter was the love of my life, but Dylan had been there for me in these horrible times when no one else was. They were both trapped now. And so was Keisha. I loved all of them. A wall of fear and uncertainty washed over me, making my knees go all weak and wobbly. It wasn't my fault, but why was I the one supposed to free them? Me? The girl from the trailer park with a drunk mama and a runaway daddy? It didn't make sense. But here I was, hands trembling, pulse racing, getting ready to face a demon.

I didn't have a choice. Not really. Not if I wanted to help Hunter and Keisha and Agatha. Not if I wanted to set Dylan free.

The thing possessing Dylan walked out of the woods, its amber eyes fixed on me. "What have you served up for me tonight, Mistress Agatha?" He stepped closer, just up beside her, slowly licking his lips with a seductive grin. "This ripe little morsel will be delicious." He groaned with a subtle thrust of his hips that said he wanted more than a kiss. "This boy wants her so badly I can hardly stand it. It will destroy him to know he's the one who killed her."

He took a step toward me, but Agatha reached out her free hand and grabbed Dylan's arm. The demon stopped and looked at her. She murmured a spell, and his wicked smile turned feral with hatred. "No," he screamed. "You will not bind me. You will not hold me!"

Agatha held on to him tightly, her own face contorting with effort. "Now, child, do it now!"

I looked at the open book, barely visible in the moonlight, and began to read.

"Spirit of our God, Father, Son, and Holy Spirit, Most Holy Trinity, Immaculate Virgin Mary, angels, archangels, and saints of heaven, descend upon me. Please purify me, Lord, mold me, fill me with yourself, use me."

"No!" The demon's voice ripped at Dylan's throat, scorched and harsh. "You will release me," he howled at Agatha and wrenched his arm from her grasp.

The wind began moaning again, gusting up leaves and dust and fear.

Glowing eyes fixed on me, he took another step closer.

I tossed some holy water on him, then looked back at the book.

He screamed, but took another step closer.

"Banish all the forces of evil from me, destroy them, vanish them, so that I can be healthy and do good deeds.

"Banish from me and those around me all spells, witchcraft, black magic, malefice, ties, maledictions, and the evil eye; diabolic infestations, oppressions, possessions; all that is evil and sinful, jealousy, perfidy, envy; physical, psychological, moral, spiritual, diabolical aliments."

"Stop it. Stop it, you stupid, worthless bitch. You're nothing but a piece of trash. You'll never amount to anything. Ever. Hunter never thought you would, and neither does this boy. He just wants your body. He wants to use you like your father used your mother, then he'll leave you, too." He hissed at me like his words were a thousand venomous snakes striking my heart.

Tears blurred the words, but I kept reading. *"Burn all these evils in hell, that they may never again touch me or any other creature in the entire world."* My voice wobbled and tears spilled down my cheeks. *I'm not strong enough. Not good enough.*

He was within a couple feet of me now; all he had to do was reach out and grab me. "You're just like your mother," he snarled.

Dylan lunged, but I sidestepped, and he stumbled past me. It was like a gate opened inside me. With those five words. *You're just like your mother.* It was then I realized he was wrong. Dead wrong. He was lying. It was just like Father Alvarez had said. Demons minced truth with lies. Why would I believe him over Hunter? Hunter'd loved me. Believed in me. Hunter knew I could leave this town with or without him. And so did I.

I was nothing like my mother.

Wiping the tears from my face with dirty fingers, I refocused on the prayer. I knew I would banish him. I had to. I had the power to set them all free.

I cleared my throat and spoke with strength I never knew I had. *"I command and bid all the power who molests me—by the power of God all powerful, in the name of Jesus Christ our Savior, through the intercession of the Immaculate Virgin Mary—to leave us forever, and to be consigned into the everlasting hell, where they will be bound by Saint Michael the archangel, Saint Gabriel, Saint Raphael, our guardian angels, and where they will be crushed under the heel of the Immaculate Virgin Mary. Amen."*

Nails digging into the skin of his cheeks, the demon wailed. His voice morphed between Dylan's and something from a monster in my worst nightmare with scales and horns and claws. I grabbed some salt, stepped forward, and tossed it against Dylan's clammy skin.

He fell to the ground, thrashing and wailing. Strange words of some long-dead language escaped his lips, but I pressed on. I grabbed the crucifix from my wrist and held it to his forehead.

The demon screamed through Dylan's lips, but I kept going. "Alastor, in the Name of God the Father, God the Son, and God the Holy Spirit, I command you to leave Dylan and all of those at this tree in peace. Leave us now and go back to hell where you belong."

His eyes flared bright then went dark and Dylan lay motionless on the ground before me.

I dropped to my knees and felt around his neck for a pulse. "Dylan." Tears streamed down my face. I felt a heartbeat. "Dylan." I shook him. "Dylan, wake up. Dylan!"

He moaned softly, but didn't move.

That's when I felt a presence beside me. That heavy feeling you get when you know someone's watching you, but you haven't seen them yet.

Agatha stood there looking down on us. Her hair was brushed back into a bun and her dress wasn't dirty or ragged anymore. Her face was clean and smooth like porcelain. The doll in her hand looked new. "He's gone, Kaitlyn. Praise the Lord, he's gone."

Surrounding her were nearly a dozen spirits. They were no longer broken or bloody, but whole. All the souls who must've died at that tree. Old Joe was there, too, smiling at me with those crooked teeth and that scraggly beard, but I didn't see Hunter or Keisha. Then suddenly, one by one, they began to disappear. All except Agatha.

No longer scary or crazed, Agatha reached out to me. "I'm so sorry, honey. I'm so, so sorry for all the pain I've caused. I pray God will forgive me, and I pray you will, too."

Her eyes were pools of loss and sorrow and hope. I wished all those people hadn't died. I wished Hunter hadn't died, and that I could see him one last time. I wished Agatha's baby hadn't been stolen from her and she hadn't died either. She'd made mistakes. She'd definitely made some very bad choices, but now she was trying to make things right. And who was I to stop things from being made right? "Of course I forgive you, Agatha."

She smiled at me, then she looked up to something above my head and past me. "Oh, my word. It's beautiful." She glanced down at me, then back up again. "Can you see the light, child? It's the most beautiful thing."

I looked over my shoulder, but saw nothing except darkness dappled in moonlight.

Agatha gasped, and I looked back at her. Her hand went to her mouth. "Henry? Mary?" Joyful tears streamed down her cheeks and she stepped forward. "Mary." She reached out her hands, as if offering the doll to a child, and then simply disappeared.

Agatha Archer was gone. By the sound of it, she'd gone to be with Henry and her daughter. Finally. I gasped back a sob of relief and happiness and pain. There really was a place we went after we died. A place where all was forgiven and we could see our loved ones again. One day . . . maybe one day I'd see my daddy again, too.

"Kaitlyn?" Dylan sounded like he had a scratchy twig stuck in his throat.

"Here." I rummaged around in my bag, fished out a partly drunk bottle of water, and offered him a sip. "Take a drink."

He heaved himself up to his elbows and I helped him drink. "What happened?" He looked around the clearing, then up at the old oak. "Was Agatha here?"

"Yes." Dylan shot upright, and I pressed him back to relax. "It's okay. She's gone now."

"I thought I heard her." He looked around, fear still in his eyes.

A little smile quivered on my lips. "I think she finally found peace. Same with the others."

Dylan slowly sat up and probed his body, a look of sudden, fearful realization coming over his face. "Alastor"

"He's gone, too."

He let out a huge sigh, and putting his hand over mine, he squeezed my fingers. "You did it, Kaitlyn. I don't know how, but you did it."

I shook my head, heart still aching. Things were still unfinished somehow. "But I haven't seen Hunter or Keisha. I don't know if—"

"We're right here." Hunter's voice was soft and strong and sexy, just like it had always been.

I stood up and turned around, pulling Dylan with me.

Hunter was whole and healthy, no longer charred or broken or bloody.

He smiled at me, then looked down and I realized I

was still holding Dylan's hand. I shook his fingers loose, guilt racking my heart, twisting my mind.

"It's okay, Kaitlyn." Hunter stepped toward me, the familiar, sexy Hunter grin making me all warm and tingly. Until I felt the chill where he rested his hands on my shoulders. "You are the love of my life. But if you had to be with anyone else, I'd want it to be Dylan."

"No . . ." I swallowed back more tears in a glob of salty mucus.

Hunter just smiled and walked over to Dylan; his voice was low and whispery, just like when the boys used to be planning some crazy outing on my night off. I looked up at Keisha. She wasn't bloody or burned anymore either. Soon as our eyes met, she threw her arms around me in an icy hug.

"I'm so sorry, girl," she sniffled. "I don't know what got into me. You weren't even with Dylan when I got so mad. It's like—like every little bit of jealousy I ever had exploded and took over my mind when I died."

Taking a step back I looked at her. "Wait a second. I'm not *with* him."

She gave my shoulder a chilly nudge and smiled. "Course you are. You just don't know it yet. And that's okay."

My heart nearly burst. I wanted to cry and scream and laugh. I wanted Hunter and Dylan. I wanted them both. But Hunter. My beautiful, sexy, always-there-for-me Hunter was dead. Free now, but still dead. "Will you take care of him?" I gulped down a sob and looked at Hunter.

Keisha squeezed my shoulder. "We'll be alright now, Kaitlyn. I can already see where we need to go." She looked off into the distance, toward the same place Agatha had looked before she disappeared. "We just need to say our goodbyes first . . . Tell my parents I love them.

Somehow let them know I'm at peace. Let them know that everything is going to be okay." She kissed my cheek with frozen lips, then went over to Dylan. Face still pale and bloody with scratches, he was crying. This couldn't be any easier for him than it was for me.

"Kaitlyn." Hunter ran a chilly hand through my hair and wiped the tears from my cheeks.

I let out a gasping sob. "I—don't—want—you—to—go." I grabbed on to him, like he was some sort of partly tangible cloud that was ready to slip right through my fingers.

"Shh." He held me close, but it was cold and wet, like being embraced by fog. "I know. I wish it hadn't gone this way either, but we've got to make the best of it now, right? Just like we always said. No matter what hand life deals us, we're got to make the best of it and do better than our parents."

My body shook with sobs and snot plastered my hair to my face. "But I can't. I can't do it. Not without you."

"Sure you can." He smiled so that his dimples sunk in like dents in a Georgia peach.

"No. I can't," I whined, trying to cling to what was left of him.

He put his hands on my shoulders, sending shock waves of cold through my veins. Then he got that voice he used to have when he was trying to convince me I could do something I didn't think possible. "Whatever happens with you and Dylan, he'll always have your back. He'll always be there if you need him. No matter what. But with or without him. With or without me, you can do anything you set your mind to. Anything. You've already done it." He gestured to his now-healed phantom body. "If you think living in a little trailer park is gonna hold back the girl who sent a demon back to hell, freed a witch, and set me and

Keisha free, then you've got another thing coming. You can do anything, Kaitlyn. And now I need you to promise me something."

"Anything," I gulped.

He smiled at me, that I-love-and-believe-in-you smile only Hunter could give. "You go on to college, just like we used to talk about. You become a nurse or whatever it is that suits you best. Just don't stay here. And never let anyone tell you that you're less than them. Or that you can't do something. 'Cause you're better than most. And you can do anything you want, Kaitlyn Karly. Anything at all." He leaned forward and kissed me, his lips like broken ice, shattering my heart.

I savored the moment. Savored the kiss. Perfect and terrible.

And then he was gone.

CHAPTER 13

I SLIPPED ON A PAIR OF SNEAKERS AND GOT READY FOR my afternoon with Dylan. Today was the day we'd been waiting for. The day we received our college acceptance letters. If we both got in, it would be off to Mojo's to celebrate. If not, well, I suppose I'd spend the night crying my eyes out on Dylan's shoulder and ruining his new polo shirt.

But this was it. My chance to get away from this town and away from our parents. Mama had a new boyfriend who helped her out now and again, and Dylan's daddy didn't much care that we were dating since he figured Dylan'd be leaving for college in a few months without me. Ha! Wouldn't he be surprised if Dylan and I got into the same school? That'd show him.

Staring in my bedroom mirror, I studied my hair. It was darker now. Still blond, but natural. No longer the bottle variety. I popped on some lipstick. Pretty in Pink. A bit tamer and more refined than my old favorite, but this worked better for me now. It'd been nearly nine months since the accident. Some things hadn't changed. Hunter was still gone,

Mama was still drinking, I still didn't have money for a car. But a lot had changed, too. I had Dylan, and in two months I'd be free from high school, and with my savings and some scholarship money, I hoped I'd be free from this town.

Grabbing the envelope off our tiny kitchen counter, I headed out the door. We'd both received a few university acceptances, and a few rejections in our email in-boxes, but this university—the one we both wanted most—sent snail mail. And I'd been waiting for Dylan to get over here so we could go to our spot by the old oak to open our envelopes. I didn't need any prying eyes for this news. But I didn't want to be alone either.

Soon as I stepped outside, Dylan pulled up, climbed out of his car, and held up his own envelope. "Where's yours?" His smile sparkled like a kid on Christmas morning.

I handed him my envelope, and he opened the car door for me. "Don't worry, Kaitlyn. I know you got in."

"How can you be so sure?" I flung myself in the driver's seat and clicked on my seat belt. Since I got my license, I drove most of the time now. And, I had to admit, I really kind of liked it.

I glanced over at Dylan, an excited, knowing smile etched on his face. My stomach did a flip that told me it wasn't so sure if I'd gotten in.

"We'll see. But this time I have a feeling I'm right." He winked.

We drove in silence to the place we knew no one would bother us: the Devil's Tree. The old oak had become our special place to be alone together. When we arrived, I couldn't help but gape. Last time we'd been out here was around Christmas, when me and Dylan had cut off the fencing from the tree. It'd been covered in snow then. Now, for the first time since I'd been alive, the Devil's Tree had leaves bursting from its branches.

"Wow." Dylan echoed my own thoughts. "It's alive."

"Alive and growing."

We climbed out of the car, and Dylan spread a blanket beneath the old oak. Birds chirped overhead. Squirrels chattered. It was hard to believe this beautiful spot used to be so terrifying.

Dylan and I sat facing each other, my heart beating faster than the butterfly darting around our heads. "Well," I said, both terrified and excited to open our letters. All these months of waiting and it was finally time.

"Here." Dylan held out his hand. "Let's trade. I'll open yours and you open mine."

Dylan had already been accepted to every other university he'd applied to. I'd been accepted to a local college and one out of state, but this was the one we both wanted to attend. If we both got in, I might actually pee my pants.

"Okay." I handed him my envelope and took his. "Go."

We both ripped open the paper and pulled out the letters. I scanned his letter and nearly choked. "You got in." My voice sounded hollow; I was thrilled for him, but terrified for myself.

Dylan looked up at me, a smile dimpling his sweet face. "So did you."

"We did it!" I squealed in a very not-me sorta way, threw myself into Dylan's arms, and we fell over laughing.

I cuddled up next to him, inhaling his scent. The Abercrombie-Dylan scent. Good and solid and comforting.

He put his hands in my hair, pulling it away from my face. "You."

"What?" I ran my finger over his lips, noticing the stubble I found so sexy.

"You did it, Kaitlyn. After everything. You did it. Things'll be different from now on, you know that, right?"

They really would, wouldn't they? I wasn't gonna be Kaitlyn, the girl who worked at the local Food Mart. Kaitlyn, the girl from the trailer park. Kaitlyn, the girl with the drunk mama. Not anymore. Now I'd be a real college student. On my own. And my life could be anything I wanted to make it. Anything at all.

SNEAK PEEK AT GHOST
HUNTERS: BONES IN THE WALL

CHAPTER ONE

MORNING MIST CLUNG to the ghostball field like spider-webs. I shifted from one foot to the other, waiting for the ghostball to appear. I caught a quick glimpse as it streaked past; the swirling symbols on the ball that trapped the poltergeist inside flared gold. The ball dodged right, then left. I dashed after it, barely aware of Mom and half my school screaming my name from the sidelines. If I made this goal, my team would win the play-offs and we'd be headed to the state championship!

It was now or never.

I ran straight for the jittering ghostball. And kicked it with all my strength.

The poltergeist energy that powered the ball didn't stand a chance. I grinned as the ghostball soared through the air and straight into the goal at the opposite end of the field.

Cheers erupted from the sidelines, and before I could catch my breath, my best friend and teammate, Jason, had shot off the bench and into the middle of the players. He helped hoist me above their heads. I'd done it, and we'd won the play-off game! Next week we'd head for the Louisiana State Ghostball Championship!

I whooped and pumped my fist into the air. I was the first ever sixth grader at Rey Middle to score the final point to take us to a championship game.

Our team captain, Tommy Lord, and my other teammates surrounded me. "Alex. Alex. Alex." They chanted like wild banshees set loose on a battlefield.

"You were awesome, X!" Jason grabbed me and gave me a half-hug, half–back slap. I laughed and yanked on his ghostball shirt, glad he was part of the team and our victory. The only reason he was even on the team was because of me. He secretly hated ghostball. Unless he was watching his home team, the Jamaican Nationals. My grin was so big I felt like my face would split in two.

"Great job, champ!" Mom plopped a quick kiss on my head before I could stop her. Oh, well, one kiss wouldn't hurt my rep too much, and we'd won! Nothing could be better than that. Mom put her arm around me and gave me a squeeze. "I'm so proud of you."

"Thanks." Still smiling, I looked around and my heart dropped. "Where's Dad?"

Mom's smile wavered, but she forced it to stay in place. "He had an unexpected showing for a client. But don't worry. He'll be there at the championship game."

Right. It was like Dad to miss the important stuff. And for what? Some stupid real estate sale. I shoved away the twinge in my chest and focused on the people still chanting my name. On the people that really mattered. I forced all my cheerfulness into my voice and hugged Mom and Jason back. "Well, I'm glad you're here."

· · ·

A WEEK later and it was time for the championship game . . . but first, I had to renew the protection against ghosts in my room. The wards—protective symbols to stop them from getting inside. If I didn't renew my wards, Mom would never let me hear the end of it. Just imagine if a ghost got into the house while we were away at the game. She'd never let me play again! Then my life would be over.

I added a dab of white paint to the pentacle on my bedroom window, making sure each of the five points of the star were enclosed by a circle, and then hung a Seal of Solomon from a nail in the wall. Perfect. No ghosts would get through that. We had to use magical symbols, called sigils, to ward against ghosts. If we didn't, they'd get inside and wreak total havoc.

I pulled on my team jersey, grabbed my warded cleats and game bag, and headed for the car.

Mom was already waiting, keys in hand. "Ready for the big game, champ?"

"Definitely." I hurled my bag and myself into the back-seat. What an awesome way to end my sixth-grade year.

"And your wards and sigils have been renewed?" Mom adjusted the rearview mirror and then checked the Third Pentacle of Jupiter she had painted on the interior roof of our station wagon along with every other protective psychic symbol she knew how to paint; never mind that Seals of Solomon and wards against spirits were also etched in the glass of every car window as soon as it rolled off the production line. As an occult historian, she was ultra-paranoid.

"Mom." I rolled my eyes and scratched at the sigil at the base of my skull, a miniature black Third Pentacle of Jupiter that was tattooed on every child as soon as it was born and blessed. Mine always itches when I'm nervous. When I was younger my parents worried that I might be one of the 4 percent of the population who is actually psychic, and that I'd be apprenticed to some psychic far away so I could learn to protect the Untouched. The Untouched. Those are the people who can't hear or see ghosts. Thankfully, that didn't happen. I'm as Untouched as you can get. "There were no breaches in my room or my cleats. All of my sigils are fine."

She glanced in the rearview mirror again. "I still don't understand why you have to play ghostball. Maybe you can try soccer next year?"

"*Mom*—" I flopped myself against the backseat and clicked on my seat belt. "Soccer is so boring. Ghostball is fun. *We* have to kick the ball everywhere we want it to go in soccer. With ghostball you never know where it'll go on its own." But that wasn't what was nagging her. What she really wanted to know was why I'd play a game where a sigil could get damaged, letting a poltergeist loose. She bugged me about that at least sixteen hundred times a week, which is nuts, because if that ever did happen—a huge IF—then the team psychic would handle it.

"I just don't like the game . . ." she muttered. Translation: I won. It was such a silly thing to worry about and she knew it. Poltergeists were supposed to be really nasty, but they'd never been alive. It's not like we were playing with people's souls. She pushed the remote and the garage door creaked open, revealing a gray sky. "Dad has to show a house this morning, but he'll try to meet us at the game."

I dug my fingernails into my hand, leaving little crescent-shaped marks. Yeah, right. Typical Dad.

We drove in silence watching the usual morning fog clear from the twisted Mississippi River. She merged onto the main roadway and gasped.

In the rearview mirror, I saw her eyes widen.

She slammed on the brakes. Our car swerved, jerking

the seat belt hard across my chest. Metal screeched. A horn blared. Glass smashed and flew everywhere. My heart launched itself into my throat and strangled my cry.

Sound and motion melded together.

The side of the car crunched down on my hip and searing pain screamed down my leg. Then everything went black.

A RHYTHMIC BEEPING was the first thing I heard. The throbbing in my leg pounded like a jackhammer. I tried to move my toes, but couldn't. My eyes were crusted closed, but I didn't want to open them anyway. Everything hurt. My body was broken.

Someone squeezed my hand. Okay, maybe that didn't hurt. I pried my eyes open and looked up. "Mom?" I croaked.

Mom was there holding my hand, worried but uninjured. "I'm here."

My leg was in a cast and hanging from some strap-like thing attached to the hospital bed. A jumble of tubes and wires ran to and from my body. Tears spilled down my cheeks. "I'll never play ghostball again." That was all I could say. Fear and anger battled inside me. How could this have happened? Why?

But Mom just squeezed my hand harder, and instead of the everything's-going-to-be-all-right smile she usually gave me when I was hurt, there was only sadness. "You're alive. And you will heal. That's what matters."

Mom slipped something cool and smooth into my palm. Her Nazar Boncuğu amulet—a bright blue-and-white glass eye that protects the wearer from evil. She got it at a conference of occult scholars in Turkey, and hadn't removed it since. "You need this more than I do."

"Why? There are plenty of hospital sigils."

Her neck, usually decorated with the brilliant blue eye, now looked pale and vulnerable. Mom glanced toward the door, which was wide open, then back at me. "I have to go. But remember, I love you." With one last squeeze of my fingers, she stood and walked out the door.

My heart sped up and battled its way into my throat. Why would she be leaving me here? Alone? Like this? And why in Solomon's name had she given me her amulet? A wave of pain crashed over me and I settled back against the stiff hospital bed, inhaling the sickening scent of antiseptic.

I looked from my casted leg to the tubes in my arm, to the window. Large, strange symbols were etched there. Psychics' symbols. Far more complicated than any seals I knew how to draw. Hospitals took ghosts seriously, especially here in New Orleans—the most haunted city in America. They had to. If one crazy ghost broke through an old ward or damaged sigil, a dozen or more lives would be snuffed out—and that was if the federal psychics arrived in time. I glanced at the small alcove I'd grown so accustomed to in my gram's hospital room before she passed: the prayer station, complete with a Bible, Torah, Koran, and an iron ghost trap etched with several Seals of Solomon.

If someone died and didn't want to cross over, the hospital psychics would be ready, no matter which religion the ghost had practiced. But only if the spirit lingered. Most cross over. It's when they don't that the trouble starts and the feds are called in. I shivered.

"Who left this open?" A nurse came in, made a tutting sound, and closed the warded door to my room.

Seeing I was awake she scurried to my bedside and

checked the beeping machine. "You're very lucky to be alive. Your father will be so glad to see you awake."

She walked out of the room with no further explanation. I didn't know how long I'd been unconscious. Days? Weeks? Maybe Mom left because she needed a break and Dad was taking over. That made sense.

I slipped Mom's amulet around my neck and tucked it beneath my hospital gown so I wouldn't lose it.

A few minutes later, Dad came in, his eyes swollen and puffy and red.

"It's okay, Dad." I forced my words through a parched throat. "I'm okay." I looked at my mangled leg and cringed. "Well, sort of."

He sat next to me and took up my hand. The same hand Mom had just let go of.

"Did Mom go home to get some rest? She looked tired."

Dad swallowed hard. "She . . ." His voice cracked. "She didn't make it."

"Didn't make what? She was just here."

Dad stroked a strand of hair from my face. "She died, Alex."

A sick, sinking sensation writhed in my stomach. That was impossible. It had to be. "She was just here." I held up my hand, entwined with Dad's. "Holding this hand."

He squeezed my fingers harder. "She died in the car accident, son. Three days ago."

My world blurred with tears. She couldn't be dead. She'd just been here, holding my hand.

Hadn't she?

ACKNOWLEDGMENTS

First, thank you readers for reading my debut novel and giving this book life. Your support is truly appreciated.

I must also thank my amazing editor, Deborah Halverson, who has supported and encouraged me through my journey of writing *The Devil's Tree* (and beyond). Thank you to Dan Janeck for his brilliant copyediting skills. And thank you to my fabulous attorney, Charlotte A. Hassett, for her sound legal counsel, for keeping me grounded when I'm overwhelmed, and for her friendship. What an awesome team! I certainly couldn't have done this without you.

Special thanks to my writing group, the wonderful authors and all-around great women Brinda Berry, Carol Michelle Storey, Kelly Jo Crawley, Christina Delay, Kathleen Groger, Jenn Windrow, and Sandy Wright. Thanks to my critique partner and friend, James R. Hannibal, for his continued encouragement; to Pat Cuchens, my sweet friend and grammar guru, who catches pretty much all of my typos and grammar snafus, and who lends her emotional support whenever I need it; to the fabulous T.J. Resler, who writes amazing *National Geographic* books for kids and makes writing conferences so much fun. (Don't stop writing your fiction, T.J.!) And thanks to my earliest readers who helped me ensure I did my best to honestly and accurately portray some of the sensitive themes in this book: Maria Grant, Danielle Miller, and Al Walls.

Thank you to my friends at the Horror Writers Association (HWA) and the Society of Children's Book Writers and Illustrators (SCBWI) for supporting and encouraging me and so many writers. And thanks to all of my family and friends who have believed in me and my writing over the years.

Finally, thank you to my father, Victor Jay Basso, God rest his soul, for always supporting me—even as a child. Thank you to my mother, Sandy Basso, who reads and gives me feedback on everything I write; I don't know what I would do without you. And, last, but certainly not least, thank you to my husband, Rick, and my son, Alex, who have supported me through the ups and downs of the writing process, have had patience when I had to write despite them wanting me to do something else, and for their endless love and support.

ABOUT THE AUTHOR

Susan McCauley has been intrigued by horror stories since she was first enchanted and scared witless on Disney's Haunted Mansion ride at the age of three. She now writes works of horror, paranormal, and dark fantasy (with a particular fondness for ghost stories). She lives in Houston, Texas, with her husband, son, three crazy cats, and a wide variety of other pets.

To get the latest news, check out www.sbmccauley.com or connect with her on social media.

Teachers: Please visit the author's website for a free curriculum guide to accompany this book.

If you enjoyed this book, please leave a review on Amazon, Goodreads, or both—it will be immensely appreciated!

ALSO BY SUSAN MCCAULEY

Ghost Hunters: Bones in the Wall

61995507R00107